Highlander's Angel

A Historical Scottish Romance Novel

MATIE COLE

R&G

Copyright © 2020 by Matie Cole
1st Edition: December 2020
Original title: Highlander´s Angel
©Cover design and edited by: Romance Group
ISBN- 9798586254344
All rights reserved.
Thank you o lot for purchasing this novel.

Chapter 1

SCOTTISH, 1545

"Murder?" Maisie clutched her mother's medallion close to her heart, wondering what on earth was happening. A moment ago, she was existing in the happiest dream ever, she was back with her mother, cuddling in to her as if she were a small child once more, and no one had passed away. It had been a glowing, joyful moment which she really did not want to be ripped away from. Certainly not for this. "But my father... he has not been murdered. We were together not so long ago. He was fine. Just fine."

Lady Lauren Nauthdon lips curled up into a very nasty looking smile. Almost a smirk which caused Maisie to presume that she was not awake at all, instead existing in the middle of a terrible nightmare.

"Well, I am his wife, lest you forget," Lauren snarled at Maisie. "I understand that you might not like it. You probably never have liked it, but me and your father have been married for over a year now and if I am telling you that he has been killed, then he has been murdered. I would not lie to you."

"But... but who?" Maisie staggered backwards away from Lauren, unable to process what she was being told. "Who would do that to my father? Everyone loves my father, they all adore him..."

"Yes, everyone loves your father, I agree." Lauren grew intimidatingly close to Maisie. She might have only been a decade older than her stepdaughter at thirty-one years of age, but she had a confidence and a demeanor that always scared the living hell out of Maisie. There was something almost evil about her. She had been nothing like Maisie's wonderful, kindhearted mother who had been taken away by a rapid illness, but Maisie never felt able to confront her father about his strange choice in Lauren. She was too shy and introverted. "There is no one who would want him harmed, nor is there any way for a stranger to get into the castle. It is absolutely impossible which means the killer must be within these walls."

Maisie shook her head hard. "But no. There is no one who would do this. I cannot believe it."

She was in shock. It did not feel right for someone of her age to go through so much tragedy. To be so youthful and to lose both parents whom she had always cared a whole lot for. It was utterly heart breaking to have to try and cope with the knowledge that she was now on her own. Much as Lauren was her stepmother, it was safe to say that neither of them considered one another family. They might have lived under one roof and acted like things were fine, but there was no real love lost there. Maisie was always under the impression that Lauren loved his wealth more than her actual father, and that Duncan Ferguson deserved so much better. But now... well, now it was starting to look like all of that was lost.

"I believe that there is only one person who would harm my lovely husband," Lauren continued. "And that is his bitter twisted daughter who wants to get her hands on her family inheritance."

"What?" Maisie almost bent double in shock. "What are you saying? I would never..."

"You killed him." Lauren jabbed her finger hard into Maisie, nearly knocking her backwards. "You did not want him to keep on living because you think him too old to have everything that he has. You have wanted it for yourself for a terribly long time. I could see that within you the very first moment that I met you. I tried to warn your poor father about your vicious tenancies, but he was so kindhearted and would not see it. Well, look where that has left him now. You have stabbed him in the back. He is dead, his poor heart is no longer beating and it is all because of you. You have destroyed that poor man."

"No," Maisie practically screamed. "No, I would not do that. My father... I loved him. It has been me and him for years. He has single handedly raised me since my mother died. I would not..."

"So, jealousy drove you to it?" Lauren relished in driving Maisie to distraction. She was clearly getting a kick out of the torture of the young lady. She did not seem like a woman who was in the midst of grief because she had just lost her husband. She seemed to be on top of the world. If Maisie could find any strength within her then she would have commented on it, but she was empty and had nothing. "You did not like it because he chose to marry me. You have always had him to yourself, so anyone else getting his attention was too much for you? Is that what you are telling me? Huh? That you could not stand him having any kind of happiness with another woman, so you killed him to get rid of him?"

"No, no, I would never..." Maisie could not stand this. How was Lauren turning this into something so complex? "I would never kill my father. I would never hurt him. I would never do anything..."

"And yet you did," Lauren declared loudly. "And by morning, everyone will know what you have done. I will ensure that there is not a single person who does not know what you have done to your father. You will not get everything like you aim to. I will ensure that none of your father's spoils go to you. The woman who has killed her father does not deserve anything. You will be locked up in jail for the rest of your life."

"I do not want... I am not after... I do not need anything..." Maisie stammered. "I just want my father. I need to see him. I want to make sure that he is okay. I cannot stand this..."

Lauren tossed her head back and laughed loudly. "You will never get to see your father again. He is gone. You did this to him. Do you not understand? Do you have so little intelligence that you do not get it?"

Maisie had no response. All that she could do was

weep hard into her hands. All of this was too much for her. She did not understand, she could not work out, she did not care about what Lauren was saying to her. She was far too consumed by grief to be thinking about anything else.

"And before you try and act like it was not you," Lauren continued, taking full advantage of Maisie's silence. "I have proof that it was you who killed your father. I have a witness."

"You... you cannot," Maisie stammered. "I did not do it. There will be no proof..."

But the words fell apart on her lips when she spotted who Lauren was talking about. Ray, her assistant who the whole clan seemed to have a strange respect for, despite the fact that he was shady and scary to Maisie. She had always thought that he was far too close to Lauren, that there could be more bubbling underneath the surface of their relationship, but she had not ever expressed that aloud out of sheer terror. Now, she was wishing that she had said so many different things. Silence had not worked out for her at all.

"I saw you," Ray growled. "Coming from your father's chambers with a bloody knife clutched in your hand." As he stared at her fingers, Maisie realized that she was still clinging so tightly to her mother's medallion that her knuckles had begun to turn a funny shade of white. "And then you dropped it in the hallway. Of course, all I could do was pick it up and take it to our Lady so that she would know the truth..."

The bloody knife appeared as if by magic in Ray's hand. He yanked it from behind his back, causing Maisie to fall to the floor in shock. She hit the floor hard, so hard that she knew it would leave behind a bruise, but the pain in her upper thigh was nothing compared to the agony in her heart.

That was her father's blood. He truly was dead. And she was going to be blamed for the whole thing. She had done nothing. She had been sleeping through the whole crime, but it did not matter. She could argue for the rest of her life, but she would be doing so in jail. Lauren would win.

In fact, Lady Lauren Nauthdon seemed to be the sort of person who always won, who would succeed no matter what life threw her way. She seemed to have a knack of always landing on her feet. Unlike Maisie who was facing this huge challenge knowing that at twenty-one years of age, it would end her life.

"You... you did this," she gasped. She spoke quietly, but it was the first time that she had really spoken out since this whole messy situation began so it was not easy for her at all. "You did this. The two of you. You killed my father and you want to blame me. You are the ones who want everything, not me."

"Then it is a good job that you do not want anything," Lauren sneered. "Because you will not get it. Do you hear me? There is not a chance in hell that you will get your hands on anything. It does not matter what is the truth and what is not. What matters is that I will win." She ran her eyes all over Maisie. "Look at you. You are pathetic. Simply a heap on the floor. Get up, get some sleep, because this will be the last night that you spend within a castle. You might as well enjoy it while it lasts. Come on, Ray. We must get to bed as well. We have a very big day on our hands dealing with a murder and a betrayal." She winked at Ray, almost teasing Maisie with the knowledge that there was a lot more between them. "It will be an intense one."

They left Maisie alone in a heap on the floor with a trail of laughter following them, breaking poor Maisie's heart increasingly by the second. She had now lost it all, there was nothing left for her. She had nothing here but misery and a desolate future awaiting her, one that she did not deserve. A person who killed her parents for financial gain would never be received well. It was a fate that Maisie did not want.

"I must go," she whispered to herself. "I must leave. I cannot stay here. I will be better alone out there."

She had never been out there before. Her father had always protected her from the outside world. He simply forgot to protect her from the monster inside the building, that was all. But he was no longer around to save her from anything, so she was going to have to dig down deep, to save herself.

First, Maisie Ferguson needed to drag herself off the floor, she needed to gather herself back up because what lay ahead of her would require her to use all of her wit and intelligence. She was going to have to carry her grief with her as baggage rather than deal with it properly, but that was the only way in which she would be able to stay alive. It was the only way in which she could avoid whatever Lauren had for her. Perhaps it would make her look guilty of something that she had not done, but Maisie knew that Lauren would make that happen anyway. This was her only choice. She needed to survive alone somehow.

Chapter 2

Thump, thump, thump. The intense hammering of Maisie's pounding heart was almost overwhelming as she snuck through the home that had always been a comfort to her until tonight. Thump, thump, thump. She could not deny that the fear of getting caught by Lauren and Ray was a lot to handle, as was the terror of making a life for herself in a world that she did not know, but Maisie was trying to cling to every bit of inner strength that she had to get her through this. Thump, thump, thump.

But her heart was starting to become something of a problem. It was beating so hard that Maisie feared it was shaking all the walls of the castle. She feared that she might be waking everyone up which would only lead her in to far more trouble than she had ever been in before. But she needed to keep going.

"Help me, mother," she whispered quietly as she held on to her medallion, just like she always did when life was hard. She had a feeling that she was going to need her medallion now more than ever. "I need you. I would like you to guide me through life, just as you have done before. I cannot do this alone."

But the usual warm feeling that Maisie encountered when she tried to communicate with her mother from beyond the grave via her medallion did not come. It might not have been a real sensation anyway, simply something that Maisie conjured up to assist her through the most difficult of times, but she could not manage it now. Not now that she knew that her father was no longer alive. Life was too sad.

"I guess I am alone," she reminded herself. "I am alone. And now I need to work out how to do that."

She had clothing on her body and some in her bag, but since she would be on the run, Maisie did not have much with her. She did not have a lot of clothes that would pass as just another normal girl on the streets anyway, everything that she normally wore drew attention to herself, which from now on she would not be able to do. So, there was no need to bring with her more than she already had.

But food... now, that was something that she was going to need for sure. Once she left the safety of her home, there was no telling how long it would be before she could get her hands on something to eat again. The cooks had always liked her anyway, she reasoned that they would want to help her on her journey... although once they heard what she was supposed to have done, that would likely change.

It hurt Maisie to know that she could never return, that no one here would want her to, that her life was going to change forever more. Although she was glad to be the one in control of that. It was much better for her to run away from anything that she had ever known than to leave her fate in Lauren's hands.

She had never liked Lauren, but she never knew how evil she could be. She never assumed that her stepmother and Ray would be killers. That her father's second marriage would land him dead. She regretted every moment that she spent silent, allowing Lauren to get away with murder.

Tears streamed painfully down her face as she finally filled up her bag with enough food to at least survive for a while because she could not help being sad that everything was coming to an end. She hated that Lauren had destroyed absolutely everything for her in such a short space of time. She might have been married to her father for over a year, but that was not a long time to shred her life to pieces.

Maisie continued to cry as she reached the front door and she slid outside, finally making her escape. The outside world offered her comfort from Lauren's accusation, but not from anything else. This was her finally saying goodbye to her family and her life, not knowing if she would survive.

"I love you," she whispered to her father. "I do not want to leave you, but I must."

As she finally took off and ran towards the forest, towards the unknown, she was glad to have her mother's medallion with her. At least that was a little bit of home coming with her. Maisie needed that to remind her always of where she came from and why she had to keep on running always.

"I have no idea where I will end up," she commented

to herself as she raced through the trees. "I do not even know if this will lead me anywhere. But I have to keep on moving. I have no choice."

She glanced backwards, seeing her home for one final time before it vanished into nothingness forever, and then Maisie focused on the forwards. That was where she had to keep focused now, where she was always going to have to look to survive. As she walked, she tried to plan out the perfect new life for herself, something that she would like. Things that she would need. A home, to keep her sheltered, a job to give her money so that she could keep on going, friends, maybe, a love life of her own. All the things that she had never been forced to worry about until now, because she did not need to survive, only live.

"Who am I going to be?" she wondered as she continued to move. "I cannot be Lady Maisie Ferguson anymore. I will have to go on to become someone new. Someone who is not known for killing her father."

Nothing was ever going to be the same for Maisie, everything would change, but as long as she was the one in control of everything that happened to her, then all would be fine. She would never give up control.

"Miss?" The morning light brought with it a cruel shake to Maisie's shoulder, dragging her from her sleep. "Miss, are you alright? I am afraid that I must ask you to move for you are in my way..."

"Hmphgh," Maisie grumbled as she forced her eyes

open. It was too light to be her bedroom, too painful to be her bed. What on earth had happened while she was dreaming? "Sorry, I..."

All of a sudden, it hit her all at once like a ton of bricks. Her father's murder, Lauren's accusation, the fact that she had run away from home and at some point during the night had curled up into a ball at the nearest town she could find because the exhaustion had gotten too much for her. It seemed that during that time she had fallen asleep only to be woken up in a brand-new situation.

"Oh... I am sorry." Maisie scurried backwards, trying to curl herself up even more so that she wouldn't be in the way of anyone. "I did not mean... I am in a bit of a situation... I am sorry."

The woman bent down to meet Maisie's eyes. Maisie was surprised to see someone looking at her as if she cared. This was a stranger with more sympathy for her than Lauren could ever muster, and she did not even know the precarious situation in which she found herself.

"Oh dear, you are in a terrible state, my dear. I think it best you come with me," the woman declared. "I will not leave you here knowing that you are struggling with something. It does not feel right."

"You... you will help me?" Maisie staggered to her feet, so surprised to have found someone nice. "Thank you." Perhaps running away was not going to be such a terrifying situation after all. "Thank you so much."

The woman took Maisie's arm and half carried her in the direction in which she was going, all while tugging a trailer filled with food items behind her. Maisie had no idea who this woman was or what she was doing, but she was happy to find out. Right now, she needed kindness more than ever.

"This is my home," the woman finally declared as she led Maisie inside. "Feel free to undress and change or do whatever it is you need to do. I will make the pair of us something hot to drink."

Maisie glanced down at her outfit. She was far more scruffy than she would have liked so she figured it time to change into her spare clothing already. She hoped that this kind stranger would eventually lead her to some water where she could wash everything as best as she could herself, something that she would have to learn as the time came, so that she could start to make a better impression on people.

"You know, that is an interesting medallion," the woman commented as Maisie took it off while she changed. "It looks like it has come from a very fine family. How did you come across it?"

Maisie did not answer. She could not reveal her true identity for fear of people having already heard the rumors about her and despising her for it. Instead, she made some sort of mumbling sound, but said nothing. She knew from this moment, that wearing it so obviously around her neck was not going to work anymore though. Not if she wanted to remain hidden from prying eyes.

So, as she dressed herself quickly, she hid the medallion, tucking it deep inside her sock, and back into her boot. She did not enjoy hiding her mother away, but it was for the best to keep her safe.

"Here is the drink." The woman handed it to her, and Maisie immediately found herself intoxicated by the smell. It was unlike anything that she had ever been given to drink before. "I hope you enjoy it. Please, as we drink, tell me more about yourself. I would love to be able to help you as much as I can."

Maisie wanted to open up to her new friend, but she was confused about how much she should share. She did not know how much it was alright to reveal about herself. She had grown up too sheltered and this stranger was filled with street smarts, that much was obvious to Maisie instantly.

"Well, my name is Maisie," she started as she glugged back a whole lot of the drink, she had become thirstier than she knew. And the drink was good. Better tasting than she expected. "And I have traveled far. I had to get away from my home, it was no longer viable for me to stay there..."

"And the medallion?" The stranger was suspiciously interested in the medallion.

"It is not valuable or anything like that," Maisie giggled awkwardly. "My father simply made it for me when I was young..." She was still too tired. Maybe even a little dizzy. "To... to make me feel like a princess..."

"And yet it looks so precious." The woman was coming closer to Maisie now, but she was struggling to keep her eyes open so she could not work out why. "As does the food you have stashed in your bag. I spotted that right away. You have what I need, so unfortunately, I need to..."

And that was the moment that Maisie felt a blinding pain to the right side of her head. One that came more than one time. It was too many times for words, the pain felt like it was shattering her brain, destroying the whole of her body, so she could not stop the world from going black.

The first friend that she had made since running away was killing her, and there was nothing that she could do to stop it.

Chapter 3

The snake crept up on the woman, she knew that it was coming, but was somehow frozen to the spot, unable to move, much less escape it. It did not matter how much her brain screamed at her to move, she could not. Something had her fixed in place, just waiting for the venomous fangs to grab her.

"Argh!" All of a sudden, a scream erupted as if from nowhere, shaking her chest, making it too painful for her to continue on with her eyes closed, attempting to block out the world. She prized her eyes apart and allowed the world to seep into her vision, allowing her to adjust to the lush green forest around her.

"I am hurt," she muttered to herself as she pressed in on her arms, feeling the bruises beginning to form there. "What happened to me? How did I end up here? Here in the middle of nowhere... with nothing..."

The woman patted herself down and stared at every

part of her surroundings, willing a memory to come back to her but there was nothing in her mind. It was like a big black hole. Nothing was there.

"Who am I?" She staggered upwards to her feet, the pain radiating hotly all the way through her as she did. "What is my name? Where am I from? Has someone taken everything that I own?"

As she attempted to walk, something sharp dug into her foot. Since the woman was already in more than enough pain and filled with enough stress to last a life time, since she did not know who she was, she sat backwards on the soft forest floor once more and slid off her boot. Inside her sock, she found a golden medallion. A jewel that seemed to be worth some serious money, but whoever the woman was, she knew that she was far too attached to the medallion to ever sell it. It meant something meaningful to her.

"Who is this woman?" she asked herself as she stroked the face carved into the metal. "She is... important to me. I can feel it. Perhaps she is a family member. A mother of mine, maybe."

The woman was a stranger to herself, so she could not yet work out who the woman holding a rose was, but she was a special woman. She was someone who needed to be found.

"This medallion..." the woman muttered to herself. "I need her. She will remind me of who I am."

She stood up once more, determined to remove herself from the forest, to return to civilization where someone would be able to help her. Since she was clearly no good to herself, and the raging pain inside of her skull was only getting worse, she had no choice but to utilize other people.

"I have a feeling that I do not trust other people well," she commented to herself. "But that is a personality trait of mine that I will need to overcome to survive. Otherwise I will be a stranger forever."

The woman staggered, the pain too much for her, until she found what looked like a crossroad. She could not explain it, even to herself, but something about taking the left-hand lane felt like trouble to her. She may well have not been able to recall any of her memories, but she knew that taking the left-hand path would take her into danger. There was still a gut instinct or perhaps a muscle memory which knew that would only take her somewhere bad. She could not stand any more trouble.

"I do not know the right-hand path," she muttered quietly to herself. "I do not believe that I have been that way before, but it is safer. Not knowing is better than knowing that I am headed into trouble."

As the woman walked, she muttered to herself, trying to work out who she was because she found the quiet of the forest eerie, but any noises that came from within its mysteries frightened her as well. Talking to herself was so much better than jumping every few seconds.

Plus, it was not normal to wake up with no memories, just a feeling linked to a medallion. It did not feel right to have nothing going on inside her head. What could possibly cause such a sensation? For her to not even know her own name, her own story... it was as if a real trauma had overcome her.

"What have I experienced?" she muttered to herself. "Who has done something to me? Why has my family not sought me out? It makes sense that I must live somewhere near here because this is where I have woken up, so soon I hope to find people and find those who know me. Someone has to know me."

She reasoned with herself that a woman cannot go through life without knowing anyone else, without having someone around to care for them. That was no life at all. She had surely had an impact on someone. On the woman with the rose. Otherwise why would she have something so precious?

"I might be someone worthwhile," she told herself hopefully. "Perhaps I come from a wealthy family. Maybe I am even a princess... or perhaps I am the daughter of a poorer family, but one that is filled with love. Either way, I would much rather be with other people than here. I do not like being alone." She chuckled to herself, but it was a mirthless sound that she had simply forced out in an attempt to make herself feel better. "I might not know my name, but I know that I do not like being by myself."

It was not much information, but for a person who had absolutely nothing, it meant a lot. It was a piece of information that the woman knew she could hold on to until she had something else.

"A river..." The woman was surprised to see a river. She could not ever remember spending time by trickling water before, not even in the depths of herself, there was no flicker of anything, which had the woman intrigued. The sound of the tinkling water intoxicated her and made her feel safe. "What is it about you, river? Why can I feel alright by your side, when really nothing is well? It makes no sense." She took a seat on the riverbank and lost herself in the tinkling ripples. "I do not know who I am, I have no idea where I am going and who I might be looking for, and the pain in my head and the rest of my body is making it impossible for me." She sighed heavily. "I have a feeling that I have been through something terrible. But why can I not remember it? Why do I not know anything about who I have always been?"

The emotions really started to get to the woman. She could hardly handle it. As she leaned forward, she stared at her own reflection, discovering an image of a woman that had to be herself but that she did not recognize at all. Not knowing who she was pained her. So much that she could not stop the tears from pouring down her face. The woman watched herself cry, it was awful, but she could not help it.

"What... what has happened to me?" she asked herself. "Why am I here? Why do I know nothing?"

Her head fell into her hands and the sobs rocketed through her body. This made it even more painful, but the flood gates of crying had opened now and there was no way of closing them. The tears were not going to stop coming no matter what she did. Whether this was normal for her, whether she was the sort of person who cried a lot or not... well that was simply something that she did not know.

"Who are you?" she cried out to the medallion. To the woman pictured there. "Please, brain, please tell me who this woman is. I need to know, I have to figure it out. What is the significance of the rose? Is there a significance? I do not know. I cannot keep fighting when I do not know which way to go."

She slumped forwards to the floor. She leaned her head on the ground, banging her forehead on the floor to see if that would bring anything back, but the only thing that brought with it was more pain. It made her sleepy again. Unusually sleepy. For a moment, she wondered if that was a sensation she had experienced before, it felt like she had already been made to feel unnaturally woozy previously... but before she could grasp on to that memory and make it something real, it slipped through her grasp like grains of sand. No matter how much she wanted to curl her fingers around and grab on to it, she could not.

"I cannot keep fighting this battle," she muttered quietly. "I cannot win with nothing."

Her eyes were flickering shut once more, her body giving up on everything that was happening around her. With no solution and nowhere to go, the woman simply wanted to remain by the river where she felt an intense sense of safety. The water would protect her somehow, it would ensure that whatever happened when she woke up would be better than before. It would save her from any danger...

Only as she slipped back into sleep, she found herself vulnerable to everything. She did not see the snake again, but she could feel it, she could sense it, it was in the same vicinity as her. The snake wanted her dead, it wanted to eat her alive. The snake was her enemy for sure.

"Do not kill me," she heard her own voice screaming out in her dream, but it did not seem to be coming from her lips. "I do not know who I am, much less why I deserve to be killed. Please, stop."

"Oh, you deserve it," the snake hissed back. "You have forgotten because you do not want to accept who you are, what sort of person you are, but that does not mean you can escape it."

"I am... bad?" the woman asked. "But... but I do not feel bad. I feel like I am a good person. I feel it in the bottom of my stomach that I am not a bad person, that I have done nothing wrong."

"Then why are you alone?" the hissing continued. "Why do you have no one? People who do nothing wrong are surrounded by people, looked after by family, yet you are by yourself."

The snake was hissing out the words of her deepest fears, allowing her to really experience the thoughts that she wanted to push to one side. Her subconscious was not letting her get away from that.

"You sense trauma in your life," the snake continued. "You know deep down that things are not right. You wish to be saved, you want a knight on a white horse to rescue you, but that will not happen. Only the worthy get saved, not those with no names who have destroyed everything around them..."

"Destroyed?" she muttered, terrified. "Ruined? Killed? What have I done? Who have I hurt? Why do I need to escape?" The snake would not tell her, it enjoyed the torture. "What is going on here?"

The woman curled into herself, sobbing as she slept, she was so afraid that everything her mind was telling her was the truth. That the snake with its poisonous fangs was in fact just the truth of her past coming to catch her. If she was on the run, then what was she running from? And how would she survive?

Chapter 4

"Anice," Bryson muttered to himself as he sat atop his glorious grey steed, Pharaoh, who was trotting through the forest for a nice leisurely ride. This was supposed to be his relaxing time, it was not easy being a MacGregor in charge of a very large clan, but he could not stop his mind from whirring. "What can I do for you, Anice? Only five years old, and you have the weight of the world on your shoulders."

Perhaps that was not exactly accurate. Maybe that was more him projecting his own worries on to his daughter, but he could not imagine that she went through every single day without missing her mother. She might not have ever gotten to know her properly because Jane died in childbirth, but Bryson believed that Anice knew there was a hole in her life. She got that something was missing. The older his darling daughter became, the more she started to understand that she was not like everyone else.

They were not alone. Bryson did not consider it just her and himself, as the whole clan helped him to raise her, but none of them were her mother. That was a role that could never be replaced. It was a tragedy. No child should ever have to grow up without her mother, Bryson believed, but fate had dealt them a bad hand. It was up to Bryson to ensure that Anice was as happy as she could possibly be.

A lot of the time, life was normal. Bryson and Anice were used to living without Jane now. He did not like it one bit, it was dreadful to not have his child's mother by his side, but they got on with life just fine. But there were times, such as this one, when the pain and guilt racked through him so hard that he found it challenging to breathe. Those were the times when he needed to get away, to have a moment for his own reflections.

"But there are no solutions, are there?" he continued to talk sadly, glad that no one was around to hear him. This was another reason why he liked to ride alone in the forest, because there was nothing but trees to absorb his words. He could put them out into the universe and hoped that things might change. "I cannot bring Jane back to life. I cannot give Anice the mother figure that I believe she needs, so what can I do? I am hopeless here, useless. I can only be a father to that young girl, which might not be enough."

Some had suggested that he get remarried, that he start the search to find someone else to be his wife, but Bryson was not sure that was the right path for him. He could not imagine himself falling in love with another woman. He could not marry just anyone. It would have to be someone incredibly wonderful, and also someone that Anice fell in love with as much as him. A new wife would have to slot into his family, and he was not sure that now was the right time to make that happen. He would certainly not marry someone just because he felt guilty. He took the idea of marriage far too serious for that.

"What is that?" All of a sudden, he was dragged from his thoughts by a white glowing figure lying by the river. At least, it looked like a glowing figure because of the way that the sun was shining off of the body. And he was pretty sure that it was a body he was looking at. That was a person. "Oh, my goodness!"

He guided his horse over to the figure and leapt down as soon as he was close enough. He stepped cautiously over to the body, his heart racing with nerves the entire time, wondering what he was about to come across here. He did not like the idea of finding someone who had passed on, he was not sure what he would do with a body considering there were a few towns around this woodland, a lot of clans that this person could belong to and Bryson did not want to interfere with other's lives...

"Oh..." But it immediately became clear that this was not a body. Instead, it was a figure. A beautiful woman lying by the river like an angel who had been sent from the heavens for Bryson. "Hello?"

She did not move. She did not look like she had been taken by death, but she was not waking up either. Bryson was anxious that he was overstepping the mark by moving closer to the woman, but he could not simply leave her as she was. He was afraid that she might fall into the water if he left her.

"Wow." She truly was breathtakingly beautiful. Unlike anyone that Bryson had ever seen before. Petite, blonde haired, blue eyes, svelte, angel like, sweetheart shaped face. She was young, a little younger than he was, which gave her an innocence look that pulled Bryson in a little bit further. He found himself intoxicated, fascinated, absolutely stunned by the woman. He could not drag his eyes away, no matter what.

"Excuse me." He shook her gently, softly, thinking that he needed to wake this woman. He had to. For his own sanity as much as for her safety. "Excuse me, Miss. I think it best you wake up here..."

She stirred a couple of times but did not fully wake up at first. As she fluttered her eyelashes, Bryson fell backwards, not wanting to be thought of as a stranger standing over this woman and watching her sleep... even if that was exactly what he had been doing. But as she did not fully wake up, he moved once more to see if there was a reason that this beautiful angelic woman was not yet awake.

"Do you know me?" The words tumbled out of the woman's mouth as soon as she finally opened up her eyes fully. "Have you come looking for me? I do not know what has happened, but I have lost my memory."

"Oh..." Bryson was not sure how to respond to that. It was not what he was expecting at all. "I see. I am sorry, I do not know you. I was just out riding my horse and I found you sleeping by the river."

She winced in pain as she pushed herself up into a sitting position, clearly having trauma all over her body.

Bryson felt bad for this poor stranger. She seemed to be going through a whole lot.

"Do you remember what happened to you?" Bryson asked her quietly, cautiously, unsure as to how she would react. "Or can you remember nothing? I am simply trying to work out what I can do to help you."

"I remember nothing." She shrugged helplessly. "I simply woke up..." She glanced around. "I do not even know where, with nothing. I have a vague feeling like I have been robbed, maybe attacked, I am not sure. But I do not even know my own name. I am scared because I have no recollection of who I am."

She fell against Bryson and he could do nothing but hold her. The guilt and pain that he had been holding on to on this day seemed to be nothing compared to what this poor, beautiful woman was suffering. Bryson immediately began to believe that it was his duty to make her feel better.

At least this was a problem that he could find something of a solution for. His own issues had no answer. Right now, this woman simply needed somewhere to stay while she recovered from whatever had happened to her, and as her memories recovered, so he could offer her that.

"I am sorry that I cannot help you with your identity," he said sadly. "But I do not like the idea of you sleeping in the danger of the forest where you may come across troublesome people. I have a castle nearby and I would like to offer you a place to sleep until you are recovered. After that, when you start to recall who you are, I will take you to your home. If that is what you would like, of course."

"You... you would do that"? She looked up at Bryson

with teary wet eyes. She could not believe that a hero had come here to save her. It was what she had wished for, but she did not know that wishes could come true. "Would you take care of me, even though you do not know who I am?"

His lips twisted up into a happy smile. "Of course, I would. I cannot expect to know anything about you when you know nothing about yourself. But if it helps, I can tell you more about me." He held out a hand for her to shake. "I am Laird Bryson MacGregor, and my castle is over the hill in that direction. I live there with my daughter, and we have plenty of room, so you can come and stay with us and have as much space as you might like. I do not know what you need to help you recover, but I will make sure that it happens." He cocked his head to one side and grinned, feeling a burst of happiness as he looked at the angel in front of him. "And I also have people in my clan who are experts in medicinal needs. They can help you."

"I am so grateful." The woman rose to her feet. She was a little unsteady, but she quickly regained her balance. "I would love to have somewhere safe to stay while I work out who I am. And who knows, perhaps someone within your clan will know who I am. They might be able to help me."

Bryson smiled at her as if this might be possible, but he was pretty sure that if she had ever been in his town before, he would have noticed her. There was something sparkling about her, something captivating, he would have spotted her right away. Right now, he was far more convinced that she could not remember who she was because she truly was an angel sent from heaven just for him. Maybe from his wife as a solution to all of his issues... of course, that was more of a playful thought than anything else, but it was fun to imagine. This stranger was certainly going to make his life more interesting for a while anyway.

"I would ask you if you know how to ride a horse, but I assume you cannot remember." She shook her head, which was of no shock to Bryson, since she could not recall her name. "That is alright, you simply have to get on to the back of Pharaoh and hold on tight to my waist. He is a gentle giant who will take care of you. And I shall as well. For as long as you need me."

"I am a little afraid," the woman admitted. "But I will give it a try. I do not want to be alone."

"You do not have to be alone," he assured her. "I will be there, I am here to help as much as you want."

The angelic woman looked nervous as she climbed on to the top of the horse, but Bryson knew that she would be alright. He had confidence that this was going to be the start of a beautiful surprise friendship and that everyone in his clan would get along with this stranger. Maybe even his darling daughter, Anice.

If this woman could help him with making Anice happy, then everything would be perfect. At least for a little while.

Chapter 5

The woman was not sure if she was still dreaming or wide awake as she clung on to the back of this man while he took her to his home to care for her. She had that same sensation of safety about him, he made her feel protected like the river had done for her before. She knew nothing about him, other than the name that he had given her, but there was something comforting about his presence.

I shall be safe with him, she thought happily to herself as they rode. Until I work out who the woman on the medallion is. Until I can go home and back to my real life, whatever that might be.

As the horse kept going, she was surprised to note how natural it felt to be on top of an animal such as this one. Inside her body, she knew that this was not the first time she had ridden. Her eyes fell closed and she tried so very hard to recall the last time that she may have been riding, hoping that it might lead to more, but everything that she could remember had a strange quality to it. It could have only happened while she was sleeping, not in reality. This difficulty to recall anything was highly frustrating.

"Here we are," Bryson finally declared, causing the woman to pull her head back, to look at what he was talking about. "My home, Goraidh Castle. I hope it is nice enough for you to stay in."

The woman gasped under the power of the sheer beauty of what lay before her. The castle and the land surrounding it, from what she could currently see, was absolutely breathtaking. The stone walls seemed to burst the skyline because they stood so tall, the lush greenery surrounding it seemed to be from a painting because it was so stunning, with flowers so colorful she was blown away.

This was where the man lived? This was where she would be able to recover? This had to be a dream. The woman might not have known much about life at the moment, but she realized that she was lucky.

"You have such a lovely home," she told Bryson in awe. "You must be the luckiest man alive."

"I certainly feel that way right now," he admitted. "But I am very pleased that you think so."

He took his steed into the stables and brought the woman inside his castle. She looked exhausted, he could tell that she was still struggling to keep her eyes open, despite sleeping like an angel by the riverside, so instead of forcing her the pressure of meeting everyone, he took her to bed. Just because he found himself overly keen to introduce her to the world right away, Bryson could be patient.

"This is one of my guest rooms." He took her to the

nicest one, hoping to impress her. "I hope this is alright and to your taste. If there is anything that you need at all, do not hesitate to ask."

The woman could not think of anything else that she might possibly need. This was a welcoming bed, a comfortable place for her to rest her weary head, nearly at the top of one of the tallest towers of the castle. She could not ask to be safer, which was all that she needed. This was a dream come true.

"I do not need a thing, Laird Bryson MacGregor. Thank you for your hospitality. I do hope that with some time, I will remember who I am and no longer be a problem to you. You have already done so much."

Bryson almost told the woman that she could never be a problem to him, but he stopped himself at the last moment. He could not start saying things to her which might later be taken in the wrong way, once she realized who she was. He needed to be careful and professional at all times.

But as he left the room, allowing her some much-needed time alone, he let everything out. "Goodnight, sweet angel. I already feel like I will spend my time missing you. You have captivated me. You... you have brought me back to life and now I can really feel things once more. I feel everything."

Bryson was shocked to realize how many years he had spent utterly closed off to the world, to his feelings. He might as well have been sleepwalking and now the sweet angel with no name had woken him up. Bryson was revitalized, excited, ready for whatever would come next.

The woman waited until she heard Bryson's footsteps

fading away, before she removed her footwear and climbed into the soft, comfortable bed. She held on to the medallion, grateful that no matter what had happened to her, she had somehow managed to keep this one thing. If she had been robbed or harmed, the villains had missed this which meant she got to hold on to a part of herself through this challenging time. There had to be a reason for that. It meant something, surely? It was important. It had stayed with her through the darkest of times like a clue she simply needed to unravel.

"The lady and the rose," she whispered sleepily to herself. "Who are you and what do you mean to me? Perhaps if I hold you tight while I sleep, I shall dream of you instead of that terrible snake. With the dreams, memories of my identity will surely return and I can finally become me once more."

The medallion was warm from being held on to so tightly and the woman was sure that she could feel the emotions connected to it zinging through her as she drifted off. She was sure that by the time this sleep was over, everything that had gotten mixed up would be back where it needed to be.

The sunshine, indicating morning time, disturbed the woman's peace. Not that she minded because as she opened her eyes, she felt the overwhelming need to smile. This was going to be a good day, she could just feel it. She reached up and stretched high, yawning happily as the morning came for her...

"Oh, I am terribly sorry, Miss," a strange voice called out, making the woman jump with surprise. "I did not mean to wake you. I am just laying out some clothing that Laird MacGregor has asked me to for you. He was worried that you came here with nothing and does not want you to feel uncomfortable."

Laird MacGregor. The man who had saved her. Who had taken her from the river side and brought her to his home without even knowing her name. He had to have the kindest heart that she had ever known.

"That is very nice of him. I shall have to let him know that I am grateful for this."

"I do not know if this is your normal style..." The handmaid paused for a second. "I am sorry, Miss, I do not know what to call you. Laird MacGregor informed me that you do not recall your name."

The woman strained her brain once more, desperately hoping that this time everything would have come back to her at long last. The sleep should have rejuvenated her and given her own self back... but there was nothing. She was just as blank and empty as she had been before. All that she knew about herself was that she had a medallion clutched between her fingers like it was all of her.

"Rose," she whispered quietly, her thumb running over the image on the medallion. "I need a name for the time being, and perhaps that is my name. It certainly feels right. Rosalyn. That could be my name."

"That is a beautiful name." The handmaid beamed brightly. "It suits you very much."

"May I know your name too?" Rosalyn asked the woman. "Only, Laird MacGregor said that I can stay until my memories return. Since there is no sign of them returning yet, I would like to know you."

"Of course. My name is June. I am here for you, whenever you need me. Would you like any help?"

As June nodded to the clothing, Rosalyn found herself agreeing to the assistance. She probably did not need it, but she also did not like the idea of being left by herself. There was something about the idea of being alone that troubled her so much. It was almost as if she had been left in the dark, all by herself for years, and now she absolutely needed to be surrounded with people at all times.

"Thank you very much, June. I would like some help. That is very kind of you."

"Once you are dressed, I could either take you to Laird MacGregor so you may speak with him, or I could take you to the kitchens and sort you out some food. You must be terribly hungry."

At the mere thought of food, Rosalyn's stomach betrayed her and allowed June to see exactly how she felt. The growl was so deep that it had the pair of them wondering when she had last eaten.

"I shall take you to the kitchens," June chuckled lightheartedly. "It shall be good for you to get to know the kitchen staff anyway. They will take to you, I am sure, and it is always better to have the people in charge of the food liking you. It is the best way to make sure you are well taken care of."

Rosalyn laughed along with June, taking an immediate

liking to her as well. Goraidh Castle was filled with the most wonderful people that she had ever met. It was almost like a fairy tale that Rosalyn did not ever want to leave. She felt a connection to the place, like it was where she belonged.

But right now, I do not belong anywhere, she reminded herself. That is something I must figure out.

When Bryson had told June about the strange woman in the forest, she had been consumed with doubt. She did not express this to her boss because she had not ever seen him looking so happy and full of life, but she feared that he had been taken in by a con woman who wanted to take everything from him. That was something that a wealthy widower needed to be wary of, but now that she had gotten herself acquainted with the lady, she could see why Bryson was so taken with her.

Rosalyn was beautiful, breathtaking, and joyful to be around. She had an aura of someone intoxicating, friendly, with a good heart. June prided herself on her ability to sense good and evil within people, and Rosalyn immediately struck her as wonderful. Someone with a heart of gold.

June no longer believed that this woman wanted to trick Bryson and to steal from him. She seemed to have a genuine need to work out who she was and where she had come from. June believed that everyone inside of Goraidh Castle could help her with that. But by the time she remembered who she was, June was sure that no one would want Rosalyn to go. Least of all Bryson.

June had a funny feeling that her boss coming to life as he did up on meeting this woman spoke of the sort of feelings for Rosalyn that he had not experienced for a woman for a very long time. The whole clan wanted him to be happy and to find love, so if this ended in a happy ever after then everyone would be very pleased for him. For Anice as well. That sweet little five-year-old girl really deserved a lovely motherly woman in her life. Perhaps Rosalyn could be that...

Chapter 6

"Rosalyn, Rosalyn, I need you to come with me!" Anice yelled, very loudly for a girl who was normally pretty quiet. "I have something to show you, Rosalyn." She tugged on her hand. "Please, it is important."

Bryson smiled, overwhelmed with joy. He could not believe how much Anice liked Rosalyn. He had been nervous, introducing them over a month ago after he first brought Rosalyn back to Goraidh Castle after finding her alone and sleeping in the woods, but it had not been warranted. The anxiety was completely unnecessary because they clicked and got on well as if they had always known one another.

Rosalyn still had no idea who she was. Her memories did not seem to be coming back any time soon, which only reinforced what he initially thought about her. That she was his angel.

Rosalyn went willingly with Anice because she adored

his young daughter, she loved playing with her and would go along with what she wanted for hours. They also spent a lot of time hugging and telling one another stories. It was the sort of bond that Bryson never thought that he would see Anice have with a woman. It made his heart swell with happiness, his whole body alive with joy.

"She would make a very good wife, you know," June commented idly from behind him, almost as if she was speaking to herself. Not that Bryson would be fooled by that trick. "For someone, I mean. A great wife and a lovely mother. I am surprised that she has not been asked by anyone already."

June shot Bryson a playful knowing look. This was not the first time that she had mentioned something like this, and it would not be the last. It was almost as if June could see into his heart and she knew what he thought about Rosalyn. She knew that he had been falling for her ever since he first met her.

Bryson knew that Rosalyn was different the moment that he laid his eyes upon her. He could feel the changes that she stirred within him. Those changes had continually grown and bloomed, every single day he found himself tumbling and falling into deeper feelings for this woman.

"I do not know what you are trying to suggest," he shot back haughtily. He did not want others to know about these feelings. "She is here to recover, not to find herself a husband."

"Yes, but there is no reason why she cannot do both," June continued, still saying this as if it had just come to her, not that she had been thinking about the wonderful couple that Bryson and Rosalyn would make for a while. "I believe what Rosalyn is really looking for is somewhere to be happy."

Bryson considered this for a moment, knowing that Rosalyn could be happy at Goraidh Castle and with him, if that was what she chose to do. She had clearly very much enjoyed her time and got along well with everyone. No one had a bad word to say about her, and she had given no complaints...

"But let's say a man had been married before," he asked June, acting as if this was not a question directly related to him, even though they both knew that was not exactly the truth. "And something tragic had happened. Something had made him so sad that he vowed never to get married again?"

"I would tell the man that grief makes us believe many things," June replied instantly. "But that our minds can be swayed and changed. Just because a man has found love and happiness once, it does not mean that it cannot happen again. Particularly if he comes across someone special..."

Now there was no way to deny that Rosalyn was a special woman. She had captured everyone in a wonderfully unexpected way, especially Bryson, but he could not deny that he remained afraid to overstep that line and to see how she felt about him. So many potential barriers stood in their way.

"Can a man love a woman who does not know her name?" he wondered, more to himself than June. "Can he fall for her fully and ask her to be his wife when he is not sure what her past entails? What if there is a man out there who she has already married? Or betrothed to? What if she has a family?"

June gave up the pretense of not having a conversation with her boss and she stood right beside him. "But if she has a husband or a family, then why has no one come looking for her? She cannot be from too far away for you to have found her where you did. She could not get far alone with nothing. A husband or a family who leaves Rosalyn as they did surely does not deserve someone as wonderful as her."

Bryson turned to stare at June in surprise. He had not thought of it like that. "Yes, that is true, June. You are right. Rosalyn is far too wonderful to be neglected as she has been. She needs a family who loves her."

"Which could happen right here," June finished for him. "Anice is very taken with her and I believe that her father might be as well. Since everyone in the clan is so fond of Rosalyn, I am very sure that everyone would be happy if she were to stay and marry the leader. It would be a very joyful moment for all of us.

Bryson knew that June spoke for everyone as she said this because she was friends with the whole clan. She had always been a very perceptive woman, so her opinion meant a lot. He was not entirely sure what he was going to do yet, he did not feel ready to speak directly to Rosalyn just yet, but it was pleasant to know that he had his clan rooting for him, wanting him to find happiness all over again...

Bryson knew that he should be sleeping. He had retired to his chamber hours ago, but he was far too restless to even lie down. Everything that had happened over the last month, particularly the conversation that he had experienced with June today, made him restless and he could not settle on it.

He knew that he loved Rosalyn, deep down he had known it from the first second that he spotted her lying by the river, and he had been wanting to marry her for just as long, but the fear still remained. He could not abide the idea of marrying her and then losing her the moment that her husband from her past life came along. But June had him thinking. If there was another husband, then he should have found Rosalyn already. If Bryson was married to her and she went missing, then he knew that he would not rest until he found her. He would not stop until she was back in his arms.

In fact, he would do that even now and she was not his wife. He felt so strongly about her that he would instantly need to know where she was no matter what. He would not be able to stand it if she had vanished into thin air. Surely, a husband would feel the same way. Rosalyn was so perfect that any man would be lucky to have her and would not be able to cope without knowing where she was.

"She cannot be married," he muttered to himself, now able to outright agree with June now that he was alone. "She cannot have a family. I do not believe that she will be missed by anyone."

Bryson still wanted her to remember her old life, he knew that she would not feel like a complete person until she had everything within her mind. But if there was nothing there in her old life worth remembering, then did it matter what they did now? Was there any reason to put off proposing?

"What if she does not even want to marry me?" He suddenly slumped onto the side of his bed as this thought overcame him. "I have been so focused on my desire to marry her, I have not considered it."

Rosalyn certainly seemed to like him a lot and he felt a zinging of chemistry between them whenever they were close to one another, but that was not a guarantee that she wanted to stay at his castle forever, living with his clan, abandoning her chance to go back home as soon as she remembered. If she wanted to, that was what he would offer her. But Bryson could not continue making plans for Rosalyn without knowing what she wanted too.

He knew that it was late and she would likely be sleeping, but since he was nowhere near resting himself, he thought it best to go and check. Just for peace of mind. He decided to take a walk through the castle and to casually stroll passed her bedroom. If it was dark and there was no noise from within her room, it would be safe to assume that she was sleeping, but if not then maybe they could have the much needed conversation about feelings so that he could plan his next move from here.

"I have fallen in love with you," he whispered to himself, practicing what he would say to Rosalyn when he finally got to see her. He needed the words to be absolutely perfect. "And I would like for you to be my wife. However, I understand due to the complications in your current situation, that might not be the easiest thing for you to agree to. Without your memories, it must be very challenging for you. So, I would like to have a discussion beforehand to see what your thoughts are with all of this."

Did that sound too formal? He could not work out whether or not it would come across as awkward and too much like a business deal. This would not be some marriage deal to create peace between two clans or to make things run smoother, this would be love and he wanted to convey that.

The only problem was Bryson had not had to convey love for far too long.

"What was that noise?" The closer that he got to where Rosalyn was sleeping, the louder the cries of anguish became. Instantly, he panicked and picked up the pace, wondering what could possibly have happened to his beautiful angel. He did not like those painful sounds coming from her at all.

"Rosalyn?" Normally, he would not walk into a woman's bedroom without an invitation, but this was not a normal situation. His poor angel sounded like she was being dragged through the pits of hell and all he wanted to do was release her from whatever caused her so much heartache. "Rosalyn? What is it?"

He was shocked to find her sleeping, battling with an unknown assailant as she rested, thrashing against the bed sheets as if they were trying to strangle the life out of her. This was not the peaceful angelic sleeper that he had found by the river, this was a woman possessed by something that wanted to kill her. It pained Bryson to see her this way, to know that she was suffering.

He wanted to end it, but he was not sure how. How on earth could he shake her from such a terrifying sleep without frightening her even more? He did not want her to be afraid, he did not want her to run.

His poor angel. She was plagued by something painful, possibly something from her past. Maybe they did need to worry about that more than he thought after all. If it could make her experience this much terror, then there had to be something within it...

Chapter 7

"No, please!" Rosalyn screamed out as a shadowy figure chased her. This had happened so often now, it occurred every single time that she went to sleep, so she knew that the person with a knife was unlikely to catch her, but that did not stop terror from screaming through her body. "Please, leave me alone."

Her heart pounded, it rocketed so hard against her rib cage that she was afraid that it might burst out of her chest at any given moment. She could hardly catch her breath because she had been running for such a long time, her lungs were ragged and sore, but she could not allow that to get the better of her. If there was one thing that she was really sure about, it was not giving up. She could not stop. Stopping meant death. It meant that knife would slam into her body and the life would be choked from her.

"I do not want to die," Rosalyn screamed backwards, using a little bit of her energy to attempt to save herself once more. "I do not want to be killed. I have done nothing wrong. Nothing…"

"You have," the snake like voice hissed back. It was not a snake anymore, the thing chasing her had taken on a human form. It looked more like a man than a beast. But the hissing had never stopped. "You know you are wrong, you have done wrong. You need to remember what you have done…"

"I cannot remember," she sobbed back. "I have no memory of everything. Not even my own name."

She continued to run. Her feet pounded against the floor. Sometimes it was the soft ground of the forest underneath her, other times it was harder, like a path, shooting pain up her knees, but she kept on going. Every inch of her body ached but she continued to push herself. She made herself run.

"You are going to be killed," the voice continued. "You will die. You deserve to die. You have to die."

Why did she deserve to die? Rosalyn did not know why she deserved to die, but she felt it. Someone hated her enough to want to kill her. She thought herself a nice enough person, everyone at Goraidh Castle seemed to like her enough, so why did this shadow want to kill her? She had done nothing wrong.

This was her past. Rosalyn could sense that this had something to do with the life that she had at Goraidh Castle, her real life, which meant she should have wanted it to catch her, but she did not. She was terrified by the idea of it getting her because then everything would end.

What if it is me? she thought to herself as she ran. My

name, and I do not want it?

The fear of the real her catching up an taking over was a real issue for Rosalyn. She was so happy and set in her life at Goraidh Castle with all the people that she had quickly grown to love, including little Anice, that she was not sure she would ever want to leave. Was that the reason she did not want to get caught?

She could not outrun herself forever. It was possibly time to give up the race and to see if there was a reason that this dream kept coming to her. Maybe it was the moment that she needed to let it come to her.

Rosalyn paused and leaned forwards to grab on to her knees, hoping that her breath would come back for her. The figure was coming, the shadowy figure was catching up for her. She was scared, chilled to the bone, her blood was icy and painful, but she could not continue to run and fight. It was not working.

"I am here." The blade of the knife, no, the sword, really judging by the size of it, was pressed against her, jabbing into certain areas of her skin. It had not yet quite burst through her skin and killed her, but the threat remained. The very real terror that something was going to kill her. "It is time."

"Rosalyn," a new voice called out to her. A friendly voice that felt far more welcome. "Rosalyn."

"Who is it?" she yelled back. "Who are you? What are you doing here?"

"Ignore that," the snake hissed, right into her ear, begging her not to pay any focus on the stranger talking. "Do not listen. You need to focus on me. On the fact that you need to die."

"Rosalyn, what is happening? Rosalyn, come back to me. I need you."

Rosalyn liked the sound of that voice, it was far more welcoming than the snake's. It did not seem to hate her like the snake did. She wanted to find the source of that voice, to lean into it, to be saved by whoever it was. Even if it meant escaping the real her for even longer. Maybe she would never go back...

"You cannot run away," the snake continued. "You cannot escape your death forever. You must die..."

"Rosalyn, come back to me. Stop this, I am afraid. Please, Rosalyn."

The other voice made everything else fade, it dragged Rosalyn away from the danger of the snake. Even the coldness of the blade was warming up and transforming into something kinder. The voice was saving her, dragging her away from hell, taking her from the truth of herself. Rosalyn was more than happy to go with the voice, to follow wherever it wanted to lead, to be pulled away from the snake of truth.

The more that the black dark nightmare faded, and the brightness of light and waking up over came her, the easier that Rosalyn found it to breathe. Her lungs bloomed like flowers, they opened up and let the air inside, and the rapid pace of her pulse slowed to something a lot more normal.

"Rosalyn! Oh, my goodness." As soon as her eyes fluttered opened, Bryson gasped with relief. Seeing her thrashing about like that in so much pain was too much for him. He hated it. It had taken him such a long time to wake her up as well. He felt like he had been calling her for a very long time. "You are alright."

Without even thinking about his actions, Bryson ran with his gut instinct and he pulled Rosalyn towards him for a hug. He sensed that she needed some warmth and some comfort. He could see that she did not feel safe right now and he needed to remind her that she was. That he had her.

"You are alright now," he whispered quietly into her ear. "You are awake. Away from the danger."

"Someone is coming for me," she sobbed into his chest. "Someone wants to kill me. I can feel it. There is someone out there looking for me, trying to find me, with bad intentions."

These words frightened Bryson as much as they did Rosalyn. He feared her past almost as much as she did. But he had not considered the idea of her past being negative, of no one seemingly coming to find her because they wanted to harm her, but now the idea had been planted in his mind.

She had been hurt when he first found her in the woods, she had suggested that herself, so that was something to worry about. Especially if it was something troubling her nightmares. There was a chance that her subconscious wanted her to recall the danger that potentially could come for her.

"There is no danger here," he reassured her through his own worries. "There is nothing for you to worry about tonight. I am here for you. I will save you. I shall make sure that no one gets to you."

Rosalyn pulled back to look at Bryson gratefully. Her eyes shone with delight, like there was sheer joy dancing through her system. "It is you who saved me from my dream. You are also the one who saved me in the forest. It is as if you are my hero and I need you."

Bryson felt a warmth travel through his body at those words. He had never thought himself a hero before. It seemed that while he was considering Rosalyn his angel, she thought of him as a hero. He enjoyed that idea, he would have loved to have been there for her as much as possible.

"Well, if it is a hero that you are looking for, then I shall be there for you always. You never have to worry again."

"I know. I can tell." Rosalyn pulled back a little bit, but not enough for her to let go of Bryson. She was not ready for that yet, nor was Bryson. He had not ever touched her like this before and it felt wonderful. "You have looked after me for a very long time now and I am so utterly grateful for that."

A thickness clung to the air as both Rosalyn and Bryson looked at one another. They had seen each other before, but never in such an intense way and it struck them both hard. Bryson knew with absolute certainty that he loved her now, there was no wondering and working it out any longer, he was in love with her for sure. Rosalyn had been afraid to fall for Bryson, her hero, while she did not know what her past was, but as he held her gaze, that hardly mattered anymore. When they were in a tight bubble like this, just the two of them really experiencing their emotions for one another, there was nothing else that could get in the way. Not even her fears or the nightmares that she had been having, not even her real name.

Rosalyn did not think about her actions, she simply went with what she wanted to do. She leaned forwards with her lips pursed, needing to kiss him more than she had ever needed anything before in her whole life. What she could remember of it anyway. She had never been kissed before, nor had she ever wanted to kiss another human as far as she knew, but if she did not kiss Bryson right now then she would die. Perhaps it was because she was still in a slight dreamlike state and none of this felt exactly real.

Although if it did not feel real before, it did the moment that their lips crashed together and fireworks exploded in the pit of her stomach, Rosalyn was dragged into reality in the most wonderful way. Every cell inside her body reacted, flipflopped, and swam in chemistry and it was incredible. She could not believe that her and Bryson had never kissed before, and she was also not sure that she ever wanted to let him go.

Bryson was blown away by the kiss. Not only was it everything that he had been wishing for, but it also answered his question without him needing to ask it in a stilted businesslike way. Ever since he first found his angel, he had wanted to kiss her, but he could never have pictured it feeling as good as it did.

Kissing Rosalyn took his feelings to a brand-new place, it took his body to another plane of existence, it felt phenomenal. Now, it no longer mattered what had happened in her past, it did not matter who she was, he needed her to be his wife. Fate had brought them together and it was because she was meant for him.

June was right. There was no reason for him not to find happiness and love a second time around. Especially if it was better for him and Anice, and Rosalyn was wonderful for both of them.

Chapter 8

Rosalyn could not get enough of this man. Her hands travelled all over his shoulders and chest without her even realizing what she was doing. She had not acted like this with Bryson before, nor any other man as far as she could remember, she normally felt shy in front of other people, but he brought out a confidence within her that she could not get enough of him. She wanted to feel him everywhere, all over.

In the dark of night, from the shadows that he had rescued her from, Rosalyn felt like anything was possible. Nothing was holding her back from kissing this wonderful man like there was no tomorrow.

"May I take off your night dress?" Bryson asked her quietly, his fingers delicately cupping her cheeks with a whole lot of love. It flowed through him rapidly. "I do not want to push you if you are not ready."

Rosalyn paused for a moment, pulling back only slightly while she thought about Bryson's question. He rested his forehead against hers and stared into her loving dancing eyes. He could not believe that he was here, that they were both in this moment, that they had been kissing wildly. He was expecting a conversation, not kisses, not her hands running all over his chest. This was utterly perfect.

"I am ready," she finally declared. He knew that Rosalyn was ready for this. The past might have been trying to catch up with her, to let her know who she really was, but Rosalyn was not interested in that right now. In the heat of the moment, she wanted this wonderful man to really see her. "I want you, Bryson."

He peeled off her night dress carefully, grazing his fingers all over her skin. She shuddered with excitement and need as he touched her, loving the electrical bolts of desire that raced through her veins. The way that Bryson stared at her with desire, with lust, like she was the most beautiful woman on the planet, made her feel so incredibly special. She loved him looking at her like that, it made her feel more like herself than she had done ever since she woke up. Perhaps she was not fully aware of who she was, but Bryson could see deep inside her soul and he liked what he saw. He liked her, which allowed her to like herself.

"You are so beautiful," he murmured as soon as she had nothing left on. "Like an angel. My angel."

Rosalyn tossed her head back in desire as he said those delicate words at her. He was her hero and she was his angel. It was the perfect mix. It made Rosalyn feel like they were meant to be together, like they found one another for a reason. For a woman who did not have a lot of purpose right now, that was wonderful news. It gave her something solid to focus on, which Rosalyn needed more than she knew.

After Bryson's hands had explored her body, he continued to travel all over her with his teeth and tongue, making her feel an unexpected flurry of sensations that she did not know possible. Rosalyn laid backwards, falling into the bed sheets, completely giving herself over to this man. She had no control over herself in any aspects of her life right now, but this was a power that she did not mind giving up to. She yearned to.

"Oh, wow," Rosalyn gasped as the pleasure rocketed through her. "Bryson, oh, my goodness..."

The words kept falling out of her mouth. What Bryson was doing to her ensured that she could not stop herself from talking, like she was praying because the intensity of the pleasure was too much for her. He seemed to know her body even better than she knew it herself, which was wonderful.

"Bryson, I would... oh, wow," she burst out as the pleasure hit her once more. "Bryson, I want to see you."

"You do?" He yanked away rapidly. "I can make that happen, if that is what you want."

Rosalyn propped herself up onto her elbows and nodded a few times. She gulped back the nervous excitement as he peeled away from her and began to undress. She was thrilled by the concept of seeing this wonderful man naked, but anxious too. This was going to be a new experience for her, she was pretty sure that it would be brand new because she could not imagine this ever being something that she had ever been through before. Certainly not with a man so tall, so handsome, so rugged with sexy dark features like Bryson had. As he undressed, she started to realize how muscular he was as well. His body was incredible, like it had been sculpted from stone as a statue for its perfectionism. Rosalyn was utterly blown away by the sight of him, she could not wait to get her hands all over him once more. She was itching to touch him, to feel him, to hold on to him while he had nothing on. He was delicious in every way.

"Wow." She could not stop the words from tumbling passed her lips. "You are very good-looking."

Bryson was stunned by this admission, he was shocked that Rosalyn was being so open with her feelings, but he liked it a lot. He climbed back on top of her like a predator coming for his prey, and with both of them naked, it was not long before their bodies connected, and they experienced a sensation of mind-blowing pleasure together. For both of them, this connection was further proof that they were supposed to be together, that fate had brought them into one another's lives for a reason.

Everything surrounding them remained strange, but neither of them could feel that while they were connected in such an intense way. It really was just the pair of them. Nothing else mattered. They could surround one another in enough love to last a lifetime. If they let one another, that was...

"You have the loveliest, softest skin ever," Bryson told

Rosalyn as he stroked her forearm. "You really are like an angel, you know?" He paused for a second, before he simply decided to say it. There was no turning back now. They had already had sex, she had to have some feelings for him too, surely? "Actually, Rosalyn, I came here to speak to you about something. I want to let you know that I love you."

She snapped her head around to look at him, to see how serious she was. Bryson was not the sort of man to say something so serious without truly meaning it, but this was such a shock she needed to check. His face said it all though, his face was flooded with love, he really did feel that way about her.

"You... you love me?" she gasped, adoring the way that those words made her feel. "Really?"

"I do." He grabbed her hands and held them tightly. "I really do love you. I wish you to be my wife."

This caused Rosalyn to bolt upright into a sitting position. "I think I might well be falling in love with you as well. My only hesitation is that I do not know who I am. I do not want to worry about that because I would love to remain in this glorious moment forever, but it is something that troubles me."

Bryson understood exactly what she meant. Much as he wanted to ignore Rosalyn's past, they could not do that forever. Whatever it was, whether it was a good past or a bad one, they needed to know. If this was what she wanted, then he was going to do whatever it took to make it happen. Even if he had to search himself to find out where Rosalyn had come from, he would do it. Anything to make her happy.

Then once they knew who she was, he would propose to her properly. He would ask her to marry him once they knew at long last that there was nothing standing in their way. Then they could go on to their happy ever after without worrying about anything. Without looking over their shoulders to see if anyone was coming for them. That was the only way that they could be comfortable.

"That will not be something to trouble you forever," he promised her. "We will find a way."

It was not long before Bryson drifted off into sleep, unable to remain awake any longer, but Rosalyn found it much more challenging to shut her brain off. Thoughts raced through her mind, tension flooded her body, she felt stuck and frozen in the moment. Now that she had caved to her desire for Bryson and there was a confession of love from both sides, everything was so much more serious. So, the intense snake of her past which consumed her every sleeping moment, needed to be dealt with somehow.

"Who am I?" she whispered as she held on to her medallion once more. "What is waiting for me?"

If Rosalyn was not so afraid that she had some bad secrets waiting for her, if she did not worry so much that she might be a terrible person, then she would simply let it go, but she cared about Bryson enough not to want to drag him into whatever mess she had made before she met him. He had done nothing but care for her, and she would not repay that with unnecessary stress. With the trouble that she could be in.

Maybe that was why she could not remember who she was and why no one had come looking for her, because she was not worth finding. She did not want to see the look on Bryson's poor unsuspecting face when he found out that she was awful... but it was something that needed to happen.

On the off chance that she was not what she feared, then it would be better for her to know so that she could move forwards without that hanging over her head. She would not fully be able to enjoy her marriage without that. So, as terrifying as it was to delve into the unknown, she had no choice now.

"Mother, I hope that this is you on my medallion," she whispered to the jewelry, hoping that her words would make it out into the universe and that her mother could sense it. "I hope that I find you and you reassure me that I am in fact a good person. That I am worthy of this wonderful man."

As Rosalyn stared at Bryson, she recognized that it was not just about him, but his darling daughter as well. She would be hurt also if it turned out that she was a bad person. Anice had already lost her mother, she did not need any more pain in her life, which was why Rosalyn needed to tackle this now. She had to discover who she was sooner rather than later. The more feelings that everyone developed, the harder that this would end up being if it all went wrong. The more challenging it would be to end it all.

"Please, do not all go wrong." She stroked her fingers through some of Bryson's shaggy dark hair. "I have never been as happy as I feel with this man. I have never felt as safe as I do with my hero. I would like to stay here with him forever. I would like to be his wife." Never had she spoke a truer word. "I love him."

    She had not exactly told him that she loved him, she said to Bryson that she was falling, but in fact she did love him. She just could not accept it yet fully until she knew her name and her truth.

Chapter 9

"This is such a beautiful place," Rosalyn muttered to herself as she wandered around the grounds of Goraidh Castle. "I love it here. The more time that I spend here, the more I love it."

To be perfectly honest, she would have been happy to forget the past completely. She would have been content to just stay here at Goraidh Castle to live the life that was being offered to her here. She wanted to settle down as Bryson's wife, as Anice's stepmother, and to just be here to live out her days. If it was not for the medallion reminding her constantly that there was someone out there potentially looking for her, someone that she needed to find also. That was the only way the nightmares would end.

"I need the nightmares to end," she whispered into the wind. "I wish that I would either remember absolutely everything or nothing at all. This in between thing is not working for me."

She sighed and paused where she was in the middle of her walk, her eyes sliding closed with the hope of the breeze washing over her would help her a little bit. Bryson was keen to help Rosalyn unravel who she was, but she could not help being afraid of that. She did not know what he would find. Eventually she knew that she would have to accept his help, but if there was any chance of her working it out alone, she would prefer that. She prayed that something would come to her as she waited silent and still...

"Miss!" A voice yelling loudly and fearfully snapped Rosalyn from her peaceful moment. She was not sure how long she had wandered off into her thoughts, but it seemed to be far too long. Something bad was happening... "Miss, you must move. Miss, I have lost all control, I do not know what to do."

Rosalyn twisted around quickly in the direction of the voice, but apparently not fast enough. There was a horse ploughing towards her, and it was coming at such a speed that she instantly knew she could not move fast enough. She tried, she did not freeze on the spot, but it made no difference. The horse had been spooked and it did not know what it was doing. It was in a state of panic and could not stop.

It banged into Rosalyn hard, so hard that she felt her body fling into the air like a rag doll. The man howled in fear and pain as he watched Rosalyn fly upwards and slam back down onto the ground, hitting her head. Everyone in the whole clan knew that she had likely suffered a head injury in the first place which was what had caused the memory loss. The man was terribly afraid that he had harmed her more.

"Miss!" he cried out as he raced towards her. "Rosalyn. Oh, my goodness, what has happened?"

The man raced over to the woman. He felt his heart breaking as he watched her eyes roll to the back of her head. The horse was racing off into the forest, still spooked by whatever had frightened him before, but the man knew that Rosalyn was more important right now. Her health was in jeopardy.

"Someone, we need Bryson," he yelled as the fear really started to claim him now. Bryson was a wonderful man, but he was also very attached to Rosalyn, everyone could see it. He was afraid of how the leader of their clan might feel while she was knocked out like this. "We need him now..."

Rosalyn drifted off away from the man's voice. She could no longer stay within consciousness. The blackness was coming for her, swallowing her up, and there was nothing she could do.

Father. All of a sudden, in the dark, a man appeared before Rosalyn. She could not see much of him but instinctively she knew that he was her father. Now she knew with utter certainty that she had family. Of course, it was obvious that there was some man in the world who had fathered her but now she could see him... well, sort of. He was fuzzy and she had no idea what his facial features were, but she felt safe with him, she wanted to step closer to him, to hold on to him, but the closer she got, the more he faded away. It was irritating, upsetting, she wanted to run to him and claim back all of her memories, but she could not. And anyway, now she could hear a female voice behind her. Another welcoming, happy voice that Rosalyn wanted to turn to. But there was no face attached to this voice. It was more just a feeling. A feeling that attached her to her medallion once more. The medallion and the truth it held on to...

As she turned around, trying to locate the new person since her father had finally disappeared completely, there were vague flashes of what felt like memories of her life. Unfortunately for Rosalyn, they were flashing too quickly for her to pick up on any of them. She could not see any of the images enough to grab them, to use any of them, to find anything out about her life. She turned around rapidly, reaching out as if she could grab the pictures and hold on to them, but they kept on slipping through her fingers like grains of sand.

"That is me," she muttered as she whizzed around, trying to reach some more. "That is me. I need that."

But eventually the pictures turned into images of the medallion. Just the medallion because that was all she knew for sure. That was all she could be certain of. The damn medallion which would torture her until she finally knew the whole truth for sure. Something that was not going to happen today in this blackness.

Rosalyn had no idea how long she had been knocked out for, but as she came around once more, she had an all too familiar pain in her head. She had felt this way once before, perhaps when she initially got her injury which caused her to lose her memories in the first place, but no memories came with it.

"He... hello?" she stammered out as she propped herself up to see what was around her. "Hello..."

But clearly her voice was not coming out strong enough because no one was paying her any attention. She was surrounded by people, but they were all staring above her. Rosalyn allowed her eyes to travel in that direction as well so she could finally work out what was going on. Words began to reach her.

"I am in love with Rosalyn," Bryson declared in a bold, loud, confident tone of voice. "I have wanted to keep this information to myself while I work out what I want to do, but nearly losing her like this has made it obvious that I need her to be my wife. I hope that everyone can support me with this decision."

Rosalyn sucked in and held a breath as she waited to see what was going to be the reaction. Much as she got on with everyone in the clan, she was not sure that they would want her to stick around, that they would be happy for her to marry their leader. But cheers erupted, flooding her with relief.

"She came to the castle as a stranger to all of us, I found her injured in the woods, and not knowing who she was, all I wanted to do was help her. I did not expect to fall in love with her. But I have fallen in love with her and I want her to be my wife." Rosalyn smiled as she listened to Bryson's sweet words. She grinned even harder when she heard Anice squealing with delight. "But as you all know, she has no memory of where she came from. This is a mystery that I would like to unfold. Rosalyn would like that as well. But for that we will need some help. Is there anyone here who would help us with that?"

More cheers and yells of agreement gripped Rosalyn hard. She was shocked to hear so many people that she had not known at all until recently wanting her to be happy. She was afraid of what was going to be found, that fear would not go anywhere, but after what she had experienced while being knocked out, she had a feeling that anything found would be nice. Her memories seemed to be nice and warm, however rapidly they flashed before her eyes, so maybe everything would be alright.

"Thank you," she rasped out quietly as she rose to her feet, staggering a little because she was still a little dizzy. "I appreciate you all willing to help me find out who I am. I have become a mystery to myself and since I would like to marry Bryson as well, I do need to find out who I am."

She smiled shyly at Bryson, a heat burning in her cheeks as she did, and he grinned back at her just as happily. By the time someone had gotten to him and told him about Rosalyn's accident with the horse, it sounded so horrific that he thought she might have been killed. That made him wonder why on earth he would not have shouted his love for Rosalyn from the roof tops already. He wanted everyone to know how he felt about her, he did not want to hide it any longer. Just as he thought they would be, everyone was pleased for him. They supported the marriage wholly, which meant there was only one thing left.

They needed to find out who she was, they no longer had any choice.

"So, I have a plan," Bryson told everyone loudly. "I have been thinking about it for a while now, and I think that we need to search for anyone who might be connected to Rosalyn..."

"Is that definitely your name?" one of the men asked her. "Are you sure about that?"

"I am not." She shook her head hard. "I do not know anything about myself. I am simply a woman with no memory. I do not know if I come from a wealthy family or a poor one, I do not know where I come from. I could only assume that it is from a town nearby because I could not imagine myself walking far in that state... I was very injured at the time, my head was hurting a lot... but again, I do not know. I am terribly sorry that does not give you much information. I cannot be as helpful as I would like."

"Which is why I would like some of my men to head out to the nearby towns," Bryson continued happily. "To see if there is anyone who is missing a family member. A woman of Rosalyn's age. Someone must know her, I cannot imagine she has been unnoticed forever." A murmur of agreement burst up from the crowd. They all found Rosalyn striking. She stood out wherever she was, her beauty captivated everyone that she encountered. "So, we can find someone and go from there. Plan the wedding after that."

Excitement brewed. Everyone loved the idea of a wedding. Particularly one with Bryson and Rosalyn, whoever she turned out to be. She was popular and lovely. There was no way that anyone could find anything bad in her past. She was too sweet for that. The only person who had even a scrap of worry about that was Rosalyn, but it was out of her hands now. Bryson was in charge of it, men were headed out to find her history, so there was no turning back anymore.

Chapter 10

"Good morning, Rosalyn," June declared, the moment her eyes fluttered open and she let the morning light inside. "Sorry, I hope that I have not woken you up. I have just been excited to speak with you."

"You... you have?" Rosalyn stretched her arms out and yawned loudly. "You did not wake me though..."

"Some of the men have returned at last from the nearby towns with news of you."

Rosalyn's heart stopped beating. A long time had passed since they all left to find out more about her, and she had lost the ability to continue worrying about their return because it did not seem to be happening. Just at the moment that she had finally found a way to relax, they came back and shocked her.

"Has anything been said?" she asked June desperately, fearfully. "Do you know what they have found?"

"I know nothing." June shook her head regretfully. "I

attempted to listen in for you but found it very hard to hear anything. A lot was said to Laird MacGregor though, so I assume that he knows the truth."

"Oh, my goodness." Rosalyn's blood ran ice cold. She could not get any air into her lungs however hard she tried. This was the moment that she had been looking forward to and dreading in equal measures. The snake of truth had come for her at last and she was finally going to see herself for the very first time. "I do not know how to take this. I would love to know what sort of past I have left behind me."

June grabbed Rosalyn's hands and smiled at her warmly. "I cannot imagine you have anything bad in your past, Rosalyn. You are such a wonderful kindhearted person. You must have been that way always."

Rosalyn would have loved to agree with June, but Bryson was the only person who knew about the nightmares she suffered, and even he was not aware of all the details. He did not know how scared she was. But if Bryson already knew that her nightmares were real, then she needed to discover the truth too.

"Do you know if anyone came back with the men, June?" she asked anxiously. "Do I have family?"

"I did not see anyone, but I cannot be totally sure," June admitted. "I am not sure of anything."

That was a feeling which Rosalyn could understand well, particularly now. She did not know what she was about to face, but she could not hide away in her bedroom forever. She could not run and escape for the rest of her life. Not when the truth was at the doorstep of Goraidh

Castle.

"Will you help me get dressed?" Rosalyn whispered towards June. "I do not know what to wear."

June could see the nerves in her friend's eyes and she instantly wanted to help ease the anxiety, so she nodded and agreed to do whatever she needed. "Of course. We will pick the perfect outfit for you..."

As June assisted Rosalyn in getting ready for the news that were to come, Bryson paced up and down the main hall in his castle, wondering how to take the news that he had just received. He was not expecting to hear what he had been told and it was taking a few moments to sink in.

"Nothing?" he asked once more. "You have checked around and there is nothing? No information about Rosalyn at all? No one is out there looking for her? But that feels absolutely impossible..."

"Is this not good news though?" one of the men asked Bryson right back. "If there is no one out there looking for Rosalyn then does it not leave you free to marry her?"

That much was true, and Bryson knew it, but it still left him a little nervous. Rosalyn really needed to know who she was, he could tell, so he was not sure how she would take this information.

"Yes, I think so." He nodded at his men. He knew that they had worked hard for him and had been away for a while, so he did not want to seem ungrateful for their work. "I think this shall be good. Thank you."

Eventually, they all left the room and Bryson was alone in this conundrum. If the second bump on the head from the accident with the horse did not bring back her memories and his men had come back with no information, then perhaps there was nothing to remember. Not at the moment anyway.

"I will marry her," Bryson whispered to himself. "And I will love her no matter what. When her memories return, we will deal with that moment when the time comes. If that moment ever comes."

He smiled to himself once the decision was made. He felt awesome now and could not wait to find Rosalyn to tell her everything. This was the day when he would finally make his proposal official and ask Rosalyn to be his wife at long last. Then they could start on with the wedding planning.

"Anice will be thrilled," he told himself happily. "She has been asking me about Rosalyn forever."

He left the room and started his hunt around the castle to find Rosalyn, but at the same time she was searching for him, so they missed one another on too many occasions. It seemed like forever before they came across one another, and by the time that they did, Bryson was ready to yell out his love...

"The men have returned?" Rosalyn asked him anxiously, before he could get out his proposal. She reminded him that she did not know what news his men had come back with. "Who am I, Bryson?"

"I am sorry," he replied with his head hung low. However happy he was, he knew that she would not take the news well. It was going to be a challenge for her to hear what he had to say. He needed to be gentle. "They could not find anything about you. No one from the nearby towns has any information."

"Nothing?" she gasped, deflating with the word. "There is nothing about me? But I must have a family, do you not think?" Bryson was not sure what to say. "Perhaps they have all been killed."

That was not something that Bryson had considered, but perhaps she was right. Maybe there was no one out there looking for Rosalyn because there was no one left alive. That was very tragic. But she was his angel and he was her hero. They did not need to worry about other people when they had each other.

"I can be your family," he told her seriously as he took a step closer to her. "I know that we have already talked about it before, but if there is nothing in your past that could get in our way, then I would still love to marry you." He took her hands in his. "I would love for you to be my wife, if you still want that."

Rosalyn stared up at Bryson with tears blinking in her eyes. She knew that she had a family at some point. The flashes of memories that she had seen when she was knocked out had let her know that much, but if there was a chance that they were old thoughts and now she was alone, then why not marry Bryson? He loved her, she loved him, and he clearly wanted to do whatever he needed to make her happy...

"I would love to marry you," she whispered back happily, finally accepting that it was time to focus on the future instead of what could be following her. "If you do not mind marrying someone with no past."

"I am not concerned about your past," Bryson reassured Rosalyn. "I am simply thrilled at the idea of planning a future with you. Starting with our wedding day. We should go and tell Anice."

"Anice, yes!" Rosalyn knew that speaking to Bryson's darling daughter would cheer her up and not allow her to focus on any worry about her still unknown past. "Do you think that she will be happy?"

"Oh, yes." Bryson caught Rosalyn by the cheeks and brought her lips closer to his. "She will be happy."

He kissed her softly, gently, lovingly, enjoying the sensation of her mouth, knowing now that they were in love with one another, fully, truly, and that they were going to be married at long last. He had known that was what he wanted from the very first moment that he found her in the forest by the river and now it was going to happen. He was going for a second round of happiness and love, all while feeling like the luckiest man alive. Rosalyn did not belong to any other man, she did not have a husband coming to find her, so she could belong to him. They could start on with the next part of their adventure together...

"Oh, wow," Bryson muttered to himself as he returned to Anice's bedroom to find his daughter curled up in Rosalyn's arms while the pair of them fell asleep together. "They look so lovely like that."

He leaned against the stone wall and watched them for a while, just smiling to himself. He had always convinced himself that Anice did not need a mother figure because she had the whole clan around her, but the way that she had fallen so in love with Rosalyn suggested differently. She clung to her like she was the most important woman in her life, and it was just so lovely to see. It made his heart swell with love, his chest heated up with a family sensation that he needed more than he knew, it made him want more.

"I believe that Jane sent Rosalyn to me," he commented as he watched them both. "It is the only explanation. She wanted me and Anice to be happy. She knew that this would work for us."

Him and Jane were young when they fell in love, they were head over heels mad about one another, and assumed that would be the case for the rest of their lives. They had been so happy to know that they were going to have a baby, it was going to be the first day of their adulthood, but of course things did not work out that way. The day that Anice came into the world, Jane disappeared. She could not survive the pain.

It was a beautiful tragedy, a bittersweet day for him. He was given the greatest gift ever, but he lost the woman that he assumed he would love forever. He thought from that moment on he would never have love again. He thought that it would only be him and Anice for the rest of his life. He also thought that he was alright with that. He did not envision a time where he would yearn for more.

But Jane would not want him to spend the rest of his life without love. She would not want him to be lonely and unhappy. Sending him another perfect woman to love was just the sort of thing that Jane would do. Sending someone to fill in the hole that her death had left in Anice's life would be just like his first wife's wish.

So, it was up to him to make the best of the situation. Anice was already doing that by accepting Rosalyn into her heart, and once they were married, he would have done as well. This was like a second chapter of his life, another shot at making it wonderful, and he could not wait to get started.

Bryson crept out of the room, leaving Anice and Rosalyn to sleep in peace together. This was a bonding moment for the pair of them, not something that he needed to be involved in, he could let them have it.

Chapter 11

"You look so beautiful," June gushed as she drank in the image of Rosalyn before her. "I have seen brides before, but none of them have been quite as breathtaking as you. The dress is phenomenal."

Rosalyn let out a little tinkling laugh as she turned around, allowing the gorgeous white flowing material to blow around her. She really did feel like a princess for the first time in the life that she could remember, her real life now, her only life since the one that she had left in the back of her mind, blocked out by memory loss, no longer mattered to her. This was the only thing that was important. This life, with Bryson.

Much as she was happy to look so stunning and to get the compliment from her friend, the thing that Rosalyn was looking forward to most was being able to call the man that she was head over heels in love with, her husband. He would be hers forever more and they could move forward into the happy ever after that she kept thinking about. Now that her and Bryson had committed to one another, and Anice could not have been happier to have her as a part of the family, all she could see was joy laying ahead of her.

"Do you think that Laird Bryson MacGregor will want to marry me in this?" she chuckled.

"Oh, my goodness, I have never seen the man so happy and in love," June laughed along with Rosalyn. "He is already obsessed with you. This will only make him more so. You are like an angel."

An angel. Those words meant a lot to her because it was how Bryson described her. He said it over and over, making her feel that way herself. Perhaps she was some kind of angel, which was why she had no memory of what happened before and why she seemed to have no family. And anyway, even if that was not the truth, she liked the idea of it. The idea of being his angel and no one else's.

"We should get you to the wedding," June suddenly said as she snapped into action. "Bryson shall be waiting for you and while it is a bride's prerogative to be late, I do not believe you are like that."

Rosalyn shook her head emphatically. She did not want to keep her husband waiting any longer than he already had done. They were both eager to be hitched already and she could not wait to get started.

"Please, take me to my husband," she replied with a smile. "I cannot wait to marry him already."

Everything was beautiful, just as Rosalyn wanted it to be. She had not been planning this wedding for too long, but it was everything that she had been hoping for since she started planning, and so much more. The best part about it was how happy everyone appeared to be for her and Bryson. Everyone wanted this and needed it almost as much as they did. It was an event for the whole clan to enjoy.

"Oh, my goodness," Rosalyn muttered to herself as she saw her husband to be just waiting for her. He looked like the most handsome man alive. She could not believe how lucky she was. "He is wonderful."

She could not stop herself from clutching to June because she was too nervous to let her go. Of course, she was excited as well, but the anxiety was gripping on to her heart and other organs. Any minute now she would be expected to walk towards Bryson in front of all these people and she was not sure that she could do it. Her knees had turned to jelly, and she was not sure that she could keep standing.

"You are going to be fine," June whispered reassuringly to her friend. "Do not worry."

"But he is so handsome, June. It is making me a little nervous. I do not know what to do."

June chuckled playfully. "Well, he looks like he is nervous as well. I bet he cannot believe how lucky he is, getting to marry someone as beautiful as you. Particularly in that dress."

As soon as she worked up the courage, she started what felt like the long walk to her husband. Her heart pounded with a deep thrill, every step making her more excited. Any minute now she would be with him, he would be able to hold her hands, and everything would feel right with the world...

"Wait, stop!" What Rosalyn was not expecting was a deep male voice to ring out behind her. "Oh, my goodness, I have been searching the lands for you, my love, and here you are at last. As soon as I heard that there were men sending out messages about a woman who had lost her memory, I just knew that it had to be you. I just knew, and I was right. Oh, my goodness, my love, you are here."

Rosalyn stared at this man in shock as he raced towards her and he scooped her up in his arms with the ease of someone who had done it a million times before. He held her close to him, the happiness rolling off of him in waves. She stiffened up, unsure of how she was supposed to react to this craziness.

"I have been so upset since I lost you," he continued as if Rosalyn was not acting strange at all. "I could not figure out what must have happened to you. I can only think that you got into an accident then wandered off when your memory vanished. Oh, I am so happy that I have found you. I was starting to think that I would never see you again, and that is something I could not have handled."

"Erm..." Rosalyn did not know what to say to that. This whole thing was insane. She was supposed to be getting married right now, moving on with the future, but it seemed that she did have a past after all. She was no angel, and the people that she had left behind had finally caught up with her.

The worst part of all of this was this man... this handsome young man had something a little familiar about him. Rosalyn could not quite put her finger on it, she could not recall a love story exactly, but he was shaking those memories deep within her brain, reminding her of who she was before. Just a little.

"Oh, but what is happening here?" the man asked as he glanced around to see the whole clan gathered in their finest clothing for the day because of the wedding. "I have interrupted something..."

Rosalyn stared at Bryson in sheer shock. She loved him, he was the man that she wanted to marry, but if this man knew who she was and where she came from, then did she not need to find out?

"Who are you?" Bryson asked angrily, taking giant strides to get closer to the couple. Rosalyn was his bride, he did not like the sight of another man touching her. "And why are you here at my wedding?"

"Your wedding?" The man tossed his head back and laughed loudly. "You cannot marry her because she is my fiancée. That is why I have been trying to find her for all this time. I shall marry her. My name is Ray Thompson and I have been betrothed for a very long time. That cannot change..."

Bryson stepped back in shock. This was exactly what he had been fearing, it was why he had held back on falling in love with Rosalyn as much as he could, but when it seemed like there was no one looking for her, he caved. He fell in love with her, and it was all being ripped away just as he was about to get married.

"Do you know him?" Bryson asked, focusing only on Rosalyn as he said this. "Is this all true?"

"I... I do not know," she admitted sadly. "I feel like I have some memory, but nothing has come back enough for me to be sure. I am terribly sorry, I know that this is a terrible inconvenience..."

Rosalyn felt dreadful. This was not what she wanted. She never wanted to hurt anyone, but now it seemed like she was in the middle of two men who both looked like they cared about her a lot. She glanced her eyes between the pair of them, wishing that none of this was happening.

"I... I do not know what to say," she admittedly sadly. "I feel very confused right now."

"You found her!" Another shrill voice shattered the tension of the moment. This time it was attached to a strikingly beautiful woman whose face flooded with relief at the sight of Rosalyn. "Oh, thank goodness, Ray. At long last. We have been searching for such a long time and now she is here."

"And who are you?" Bryson asked wearily. "Are there any more people coming to interrupt my day?"

"I am Lauren, Ray's sister," she said with a delighted smile. Lauren stuck her hand out for Bryson to shake which he did wearily. "It is good to meet you. Thank you so much for taking care of my sister in law."

Bryson was silent for a beat too long as he let this wash over him. This was not supposed to be happening, this was more like a nightmare than real life, but since it was the truth, he had to do something about it. He darted his eyes to look at everyone, but the guests to his wedding could hardly meet his eyes. The only person staring back at him was Anice, and his poor daughter looked terrified.

She had already been through enough in her life. He could not make her witness this as well.

"Let us halt the wedding," he finally declared quietly. "We must go and discuss this in the other room."

Those words made Rosalyn really anxious. She had a terrible feeling that if this wedding got stopped now so they could sort this mess out, then it would never happen... but she could not be the terrible person who refused to talk to this man and his sister who had searched for her for a long time.

"Yes, that is a good idea," Lauren declared as she made a strange sweeping gesture with her hands. "We should straighten this whole mess out so that the three of us can all go back home."

Three. Rosalyn sucked in a deep and panicked breath. The three included her. She never wanted to leave this castle, this place, this clan... how could she ensure that she stayed? Rosalyn tried to catch Bryson's eyes, to see if he would be willing to help her stay, but his eyes were firmly fixed on the floor like he could not stand to look at her any longer. He had already fallen out of love with her, he did not want to see her any longer, he was ready to kick her out at the first opportunity. This was hopeless.

Her eyes whizzed around to see Ray instead and he was grinning at her like the cat who had the cream. She could see that he was so pleased to have found her, that he had missed her like crazy, that he wanted her back. She should have felt excited about that, but it only upset her because she was afraid to leave behind the only life that she knew. Sure, she might be heading in to one that she lived before, but she did not know a damn thing about it.

She was dressed up like a bride, like a princess, but it

seemed that her happy ever after was not going to happen in the way that she wanted.

Chapter 12

"Oh, it has been such a terrible time for us," Lauren started as soon as the four of them were alone in one of Bryson's biggest halls. "We have been missing our darling for such a long time. Especially my brother, Ray. He has been bereft without the love of his life. It has been so challenging."

"My men went out looking," Bryson growled, his anger at how unfair the situation was, was really getting to him now. "They searched all the nearby towns and no one knew a woman who had gone missing."

"Clearly, they did not make it to us," Lauren shot back without a pause. "We did not have any visitors to our town. It was only because my brother has been looking for his love so fiercely that he happened up on the rumors and thank goodness as well. I cannot express how worried we have been."

Rosalyn's stomach churned. She feared that she might throw up at any given moment. The dress that she had put on so excitedly this morning, proud to finally make all of her romantic dreams come true, was slowly becoming a symbol of failure. It was going to be a reminder of her losing everything.

"My darling, Maisie, has been a huge loss to me, and to our clan," Ray interjected. "Everyone has missed her. They will be so pleased to know that we can finally bring her back to where she is meant to be…"

"Wait, Maisie?" All of a sudden, the name Rosalyn slipped off her like a coat that never quite fit her in the first place. It had not shaken a lot, but there was a definite memory within her. "Is that me?"

"Oh, my dear." Ray cocked his head to one side and shot her a sympathetic look. He seemed to see her pain. "You do not even recall your own name? No wonder you have struggled to find your way home. You are Lady Maisie Ferguson. Daughter of Laird Duncan Ferguson and Lady Tara Ferguson…"

"Although unfortunately, the pair of them were killed in an accident years ago," Lauren jumped in through gritted teeth. It was obvious she did not want Maisie to find out about her parents in such a brutal way. "Which is why it has been so hard on the people that you have gone missing as well."

Maisie… it felt right. She knew instinctively that name belonged to her. She also had a vague recognition of the names given to her for her parents. They belonged to her and she knew it. It was just a horrible shame to learn that they were no longer alive. She so wanted to see them, to hold them.

"I cannot find memories of my mother," she admitted, talking more to herself than anyone else. "But my father... he loved me. I can feel it deep within me. He loved me a lot and wanted the best for me..."

"Which is why he was happy for you to marry Ray," Lauren insisted. "He was chosen for you because your father just knew that he could look after you. He wanted the best for you always."

Lauren's words were growing worse with every passing second. Maisie did not know how to take them. If Ray was who her father, who clearly adored her, wanted her to marry, and she had agreed to it, then how could she ignore that now? How could she ignore his wish? Sure, she had fallen in love with Bryson while she had been staying with him, but that was not real life. Bryson did not even know her real name. They had been more playing a game where she was an angel and he was her hero. But none of it was real.

Now, he could not even look at her. Bryson was disgusted by her and who she really was.

"It is terrible to learn that you do not remember anything." Lauren grew nearer to Maisie and stared deep into her eyes. Maisie's initial reaction was to pull away because she did not really want this stranger to see her... but the woman knew her better than she knew herself. She had no choice. "But you have clearly been cared for very well. I am sure that my brother and everyone in our town will be pleased to know that. However, it really is time for us to leave. You are supposed to be married to my brother already. We do not wish to put it off any longer. I am sure that you feel the same way, do you not?"

Maisie did not know what to say. She was nowhere near eager to marry the man that she did not know, but she also could not follow through her plan to get hitched to Bryson either. Not when he did not want her. "I cannot just immediately leave. I have people here who I must say goodbye to..."

"They do not know the real you, Maisie." Lauren was beginning to become visibly irritated. "They do not wish to say farewell to a woman that does not exist. I believe that you have imposed on these kind people for long enough. You are starting to take advantage of their hospitality..."

Lauren tried to grab hold of Maisie's arm, to speed up the process of them leaving, but Maisie was too afraid to comply. She snatched away, knowing that while she should trust these people, she did not. Not yet. There was something in the pit of her stomach screaming at her not to. Probably her love for Bryson.

She was torn. She wanted to stay and live out the fantasy that she had created for herself with Bryson. She wanted to be his wife, to spend more time with Anice, to be happy here, but how could she when everything that these people knew about her was a lie? She could not do it...

"I have been afraid," she declared quietly. "Worried that someone has been after me. A nightmare..."

"Oh, Maisie, my love." Ray grabbed Maisie's hands. "You have been suffering from nightmares ever since your parents died in the accident. You have held on to a lot of guilt for that."

"Wh... why?" she stammered back, terrified of the answer. "Was it my fault?"

"No one else believes that it was your fault. Only you. We all believe you to be innocent...."

"Best not upset her," Lauren jumped in once more, controlling the conversation as much as she could. "That is something we need not discuss here. We can look after Maisie when we get home..."

As the three of them talked... well, it was more Lauren talking at the other two, Bryson paced up and down the room like a caged animal. He felt a bit like a tiger than wanted to escape his entrapment but could not. There was something wholly wrong about this whole situation, but he could not figure out what.

Ray and Lauren really did seem to know Rosalyn, or Maisie as it now seemed that she was called, and they had a lot of information on her, but it did not feel right. Were they spouting nonsense at her and she was so desperate for any memories that she would go along with anything? Even if it meant being pulled away from him and their love on their wedding day of all times as well?

Urgh, it would not have surprised him. He instantly got a bad feeling from them. Lauren was bossy and seemed to have a passive aggressive nasty streak. He did not enjoy her company immediately. And as for Ray... he was pompous and stupid. Bryson could not imagine Rosa... Maisie, liking him one bit.

But if she had promised her father that she would marry him, then maybe she felt like she was obligated to. Many families arranged husbands for their children, it was certainly not unheard of. Bryson did not have to like it for it to become reality. He had been afraid of something like this happening, but he never imagined that it would hurt so much when it did. He felt like he was breaking into pieces.

What shall I do? he asked himself anxiously. I still love this woman and want to marry her, no matter what her name is or where she has come from... but who does she want to marry?

He needed to take action, to do something. After all, this was his castle, his kingdom. He held all the rights in this place so if he wanted to kick these people out then he would. Then he could continue on with his wedding day, but he did not want to put the love of his life through anything that she did not want.

If she wished to leave with these people, to return to the life that she had before, then he had no choice but to say goodbye to his second chance at happiness. This would probably hurt more than Jane though because she had no choice but to leave him. Maisie would be making that decision.

I might not be destined for happiness. That thought crushed him, but it was potentially all too real.

"Do you need time?" Bryson's voice boomed, causing everyone to stop talking for a moment, even Lauren. "Do you need time to make a decision about what you wish to do? You do not have to choose now."

"But we have a life to get back to." Lauren's hands flung on to her hips. "My brother has wanted his fiancée back for a very long time. You cannot expect him to wait any longer."

"But this is all brand new for Rosalyn... I mean Maisie." Bryson noted how Lauren laughed nastily as he got her name wrong. Maisie would take some getting used to for sure. "She might well be overwhelmed and need some time to adjust. And as she has expressed, she wished to say goodbye to people..."

"I will not have you trying to kidnap her," Lauren snarled. "You want to claim her for your own, do you not? Is that not why you were trying to marry her today? Well, she is betrothed to Ray and that is who she shall marry. There is nothing you can do to prevent that from happening. I suggest you stop right away."

"That is not what I am doing." Bryson could feel the heat creeping into his cheeks. "Not at all. I just want what is best for everyone involved. This is a very strange time and I want to know what Maisie wishes for."

They all turned to look at Maisie who was honestly far too speechless to say anything. She did not know where to even begin. She felt like she was being pulled in a hundred different directions and she was not sure which way to turn. As much as she would have loved to remain in her fantasy with Bryson, she was also a little bit intrigued about the life that had come before, about who she was. She could not see herself falling in love with Ray, she felt weird in his presence right now, but he did seem to love her too...

"I do not know what I want," she admitted quietly. "I am very confused right now."

Bryson did not want to let her go. He wanted to hold on to her forever more.

Lauren was determined to drag her along with her no matter what.

Ray looked like a man who needed his fiancée back at

any cost.

    Maisie simply wished that these people had turned up a little while later when she was already married. Then it would be too late to take her from her utopia. She would be able to live in it forever without a worry in the world about who she did or did not agree to wed in the past life that she did not remember.

Chapter 13

"I think that I am going to need proof," Bryson suddenly shouted out as a last-ditch attempt to stop these people from taking the love of his life away from him. "I need to see that you do know Maisie properly."

"We have given you all of the proof that we have." Ray shrugged his shoulders helplessly. "You have seen that Maisie knows us. As soon as her true name was mentioned, it sparked memories. She knows that her father loved her more than anything in the world, she recognizes us, you can see it."

Bryson darted his eyes over to Maisie, but it crushed him to see her with shining tears in her gaze. He knew that was from her confusion because she was so afraid of knowing these people. But she did know them. Yet he could not help thinking that the nightmares seemed far more significant than anyone was letting on. Maisie was traumatized by these dreams. They came from fear, not guilt.

"Well, hang on a minute." Lauren rested her hand on her brother's shoulder to push him behind her. Bryson could not stand to see her pushing everyone around like she was the queen of the world. He did not know how they stood it as well. "There is something. There is the engagement gift that you gave Maisie."

Everyone looked a little confused at that moment. Maisie had been found with nothing, certainly no sign of a ring or Bryson would have immediately known that she belonged to someone else...

"A medallion," Lauren continued. "A golden medallion that Maisie has always worn around her neck, although I do not see it right now." She narrowed her eyes at Maisie. "But it is engraved with a picture of your mother and a flower. You must know what I am speaking of, it is so important to you."

Maisie bent down slowly and pushed her fingers into her shoe to retrieve the medallion. She did sometimes wear it around her neck these days, but since she had been found with it in her shoe, there was a comfort to having it by her foot. She wanted it there on her wedding day as a reminder of how she had been found. She needed the memory of how Bryson had met her. But now... well, now the medallion had taken on a whole new meaning for her. It actually linked her to the man she had previously been engaged to. The man who was staring at her expectantly, needing something from her.

"I always felt like this picture was of my mother," she half whispered as she looked at the engraved image once more. "It has always been important to me. I knew that when I first saw it."

Lauren's eyes lit up in delight as she spotted the medallion. She knew that she had Maisie finally seeing everything that she was trying to tell her. The medallion was the key to everything, it was the answer.

"Ah, I knew that you would have it!" Lauren clapped her hands together in excitement. "I knew that you would not let that go. You have loved it ever since my brother got it made especially for you. I believe that is the moment when you fully allowed yourself to be loved by him. Before then, the guilt that you have experienced has held you back and made you feel like you are not worthwhile."

Maisie could not ignore the fact that she did feel a bit like that, even with Bryson. As incredible as he made her feel, there was always a little part of her that was not sure she deserved him. She had always been worried that she was a bad person and that he deserved better.

"It is just a shame," Ray jumped in. "That it was not long after you finally accepted my love that you vanished into thin air, leaving me absolutely heartbroken. But now you are here. I get to have you again."

Maisie span the medallion around in her fingers, over and over again, wishing that she could remember her mother. Clearly this woman was very important to her, so important that her fiancé got her engraved into a medallion for her, yet she could not recall her at all. It was very frustrating. This whole memory loss thing was rather annoying. All she wanted to do was to know exactly who she was. Why was that so hard?

"I know that this must be a lot for you," Lauren continued, still on the mission to make Maisie understand everything. "But I believe that your memories will not return fully while you are in a strange environment. Once we get you home, everything will come back to you. Maybe then we can even unravel the mystery of what happened to you in the first place. We do not want you to go missing again."

Maisie nodded slightly because she knew that Lauren was right. But if she left with her and Ray then there was a massive chance that she would never see Bryson again for her whole life. Her husband was hardly going to let her come and visit the man that she nearly got hitched to with memory loss, was he? She would never get to see her friends again either, even Anice would eventually forget all about her.

She would not just be headed back to her home, she would also be saying a final farewell to the wonderful fantasy that she had been living in. She would be losing it all.

"Your family has always been very big on honor," Ray reminded her with a cocked eyebrow. It was almost as a warning rather than a simple reminder. "And your father said that it would be an honor for me to take you as my wife. I do not want to let him down and I am sure that you feel the same way."

Maisie knew that her father loved her a lot, that was one of the true facts that she could hold on to, and she was sure that she would have done whatever he wanted of her when he was alive... including this.

She tried to hold back the tears as she nodded, but she did not succeed. Her cheeks covered in wetness. This was the outcome that it seemed had to happen, even if it was not what she wanted.

"I am sorry," she said with great regret to Bryson. "If this is what I have promised my father..."

"I understand," he instantly snapped back. Whether that statement was true or not, he had not yet decided, but it hardly mattered. She had chosen what she wanted to do. She had picked him and there was nothing that he could do about it. As much as he wanted to, there was not a damn thing. "You have promised yourself to this man..." Bryson could not bring himself to say the man's name aloud. "There is nothing that can be done about that. I understand that you must leave and nothing can be done."

Those words shattered Maisie even more. There was a part of her that wanted Bryson to fight for her, to refuse to let her go. But he was giving up, leaving her to go with these people. It was the noble thing to do, which of course was why he was doing it, being the great man that he was, but still it hurt.

Insist that you stay, Maisie's brain unhelpfully screamed at her. Do not go. You cannot.

But it was too late. Lauren had already taken control of the situation. She was already insisting that it was time for the three of them to get moving so that Maisie could marry Ray. It was all moving far too fast for her liking. She was spinning around, the world was twisting and turning much too quickly, and she could not get off. Bryson was slipping through her fingers like grains of sand and she could not grasp on to him however much she wanted to. He was pulling away from her, separating, because he needed to. For his own sake. He could not be near Maisie knowing that he was losing her.

"I need my things," Maisie whispered. "From my bedroom here. I have things…"

"Those things are not yours," Lauren replied in a sickly-sweet voice. It was clear that she had started to lose patience with Maisie now. "They have been leant to you while you have been here, but they are not for you to permanently keep. You have your own things at home and we should get to them now."

"But this dress," she insisted, not quite ready to give up her life here just yet. "I cannot return home in a wedding dress. The clan will not be happy to know that I was about to marry another man."

"You do not need to worry about so many things." Lauren's hand curled around Maisie's arm hard. "If my darling brother can forgive you for what you have done while you have no memory, then everyone else will follow. Plus, if it is that much of a problem, I can lend you something of mine to wear. But we must not stay here for another second longer because we will start to become a nuisance. Is that what you wish for? For Laird Bryson MacGregor who has been so kind to you, to remember you as a nuisance?"

Of course, that was not what Maisie wanted. She would come away from this with only good memories of Bryson and everyone else, so she wished them to have the same of her.

"No, of course not," she replied meekly. "Let us leave now before everything can get worse."

June was the only person that Maisie really got a chance to say goodbye to. Bryson could not seem to stand the idea of being close to her at all, and Anice was nowhere to be seen. Maisie could only assume that she was being kept far away from the chaos, and rightly so. The poor girl was only five years old and did not need this heartbreak. Maisie was not sure what she would have said to her anyway. There was no way to explain that although they had a wonderful bond, she needed to leave.

"I am so sorry that you are leaving, Rosalyn," June whispered with tears in her eyes. "I shall so miss having you around. I was looking forward to having a friend forever. We have shared some lovely times."

"It is Maisie now," she replied through her own sadness. "I can feel that I am a Maisie, but none of this feels real to me. I cannot explain it, it is all so very strange. I cannot get my head around it. I suppose this is an outcome that I should have been expecting, but still it feels odd to know that I am betrothed to Ray."

June would not say it aloud, but she could not believe it either. Ray and Lauren instantly gave her the chills. They were the sort of people that she would personally choose to keep far away from. She did not like the idea of sending off her Rosalyn with them. But she was a lowly hand maiden who could not have a say in such matters. It did not seem to be her right to get involved with any of this.

Of course, June also held on to the added guilt that she pushed Bryson towards the woman that he so clearly loved. He was hesitant to take action and she guided him towards her. She told him that it was the right thing to do, and clearly she was mistaken about that.

Her heart was breaking because she had sent him in

Rosalyn's direction and now there was a large chance that he would crumble because of her.

Chapter 14

"I love you, my sweet Maisie," Ray said with a whisper, almost as if he was trying to antagonize Bryson. Bryson's fists curled around in anger. He could not stand to hear someone else telling his woman that he loved her. Bryson was the one who loved her, no one else could love her like he did, yet he was the one losing out. It was utterly infuriating. "I do love you and I cannot wait to get you home."

"I have to respect this," he hissed to June. "I do not like it, but I must respect it. It is what Maisie has chosen. She wants to respect her father's wishes, so she is headed back home. Away from me."

"I am so terribly sorry that you feel this way," June replied sadly. "I do feel utterly terrible that you have had your heart broken once more. A man like you does not deserve this sort of tragedy. Again."

Bryson felt like he was dying inside. Every passing second was more painful than the last. June's words only made it harder to swallow but he did not have a choice in the matter. The idea of even more tragedy falling over him and Anice as well was utterly overwhelming for him. His daughter was going to be heart broken. She was not with him right now but soon he would have to explain everything to her.

The carriage for Maisie was waiting outside of the castle walls. Bryson followed behind. Not because he wanted to see her leave, but because he needed to. He did not have any choice but to watch her go because he had to check that it was real. A lot of this felt like a nightmare to him that he could not escape.

"Well, I suppose this is goodbye," Lauren declared with a smile so wide it seemed almost sinister. "Thank you again for looking after our girl. It has been much appreciated and of course, we are sorry to come when we did. I know that this must be a bit of a disappointment to you, but you will be pleased to know that my brother will take very good care of his fiancé. Their marriage will be a good one."

Perhaps she meant those words to be kind, but to Bryson they felt evil, like she wanted to sicken him. Bryson just about managed to nod but he could not get out any words. He feared that if he started to speak then, all of his feelings towards Maisie would come spilling out and he would not be able to stop them. Unfortunately, they were passed that now. There was no use in saying anything.

"Yes, we will have an amazing marriage, Maisie." He pulled her a little too close to him. She obviously was not comfortable with it just yet but did not complain. "The absolute best. I am going to treat you like the princess that you deserve to be treated and if your memories come back... then all the better."

"Being at my home will help me," Maisie muttered helplessly. "I am sure to recall everything."

But she did not think that all the memories in the world would erase what she had shared with Bryson. She could not picture anything feeling as strong and powerful. Saying farewell to him, silently as she had not really been given the chance to express it to him properly, was going to kill her.

"Let us get into the carriage," Ray insisted, now needing to speed things along even more. "There are so many people wanting to see you, Maisie, we must not keep them waiting any longer."

A wave of guilt washed over Maisie. Here she was, selfishly wishing that she never had to go back home and there were people there who were missing her and wanted to know what had happened to her. She could not continue thinking only of herself. This was what she needed to do. So, she allowed Ray to assist her as she climbed into the carriage, and she mentally said goodbye to the only love she had ever known.

Ray and Lauren were keen to get going. There was no waiting around, they insisted on making the carriage go immediately, so Maisie was not given much time to twist around in her seat to wave goodbye to Bryson. But she got a moment, and that was enough to shatter her heart. The best day of her life had far too rapidly become her worst and Maisie was all cut up about it, unable to recover.

A stray tear lurched down her cheek. Now, she would not get to marry the man that she wanted to. Instead, she was going to be stuck with a stranger who she did not feel much for at all. She supposed that she must have done before her memories vanished, she must have felt a lot for him to agree to marry him, but she could not conjure up any of that now. It was almost as if she did not like him.

No, I must love him, she thought to herself as she tried to accept her reality. I must have felt for him as I do Bryson or I never would have agreed to be his wife. We must have kissed and... and...

But the idea of kissing Ray, never mind anything else, was almost overwhelming for her. She certainly could not picture a world where she would want to start a family with Ray... but she had to trust what her father had put forth for her. She had to believe that he would want the best for her and that he truly believed Ray to be the best man. Who knew, maybe she would fall back in love with Ray and everything would end up perfect after all. Maybe this was just a blip in the love story that she was destined to have.

She sighed heavily and leaned back against the seat, her eyes flickering with sadness as she did. She expected Ray to keep on with the sympathy that he had been giving her for her complex situation, but he said nothing. Maisie was not expecting anything from Lauren because she was clearly irritated by her, but she was the one who ended up speaking to Maisie, leaning forward as she did.

"Maisie, you cannot be sad about that man. He did not care for you, I can assure you."

Maisie's eyes snapped open. "What do you mean? Did

he say something about me?"

Lauren sniffed nastily. "He did not need to. I could see it. I have always been a very good judge of character. I believe that Bryson knew who you were all along. He was trying to marry you for your inheritance. The name Maisie Ferguson is a well-known one. Your father was a well-known man. Suitors from all around the country wanted to marry you, which is why your father felt the need to intervene. He chose a very good man for you. You should be happy that you have ended up with Ray."

Maisie did not know how to swallow this information down. So, now she was just finding out that she was wealthy? That she had a lot of family money? That people wanted to marry her? In which case, it was very unusual that no one had noticed her missing. She found that odd. Unless...

Did Bryson lie to her? Did he only pretend to send out men to find out information because all along he wanted to marry her for money? Even if he did not seem like someone who needed anything. Maybe he was hiding a lot from her the whole time. That was why he did not wait until her memories returned...

No, she told herself firmly. It does not matter what Lauren thinks of Bryson. You know the truth.

She did know the truth as well. She did understand Bryson, there was no doubt about it. He loved her, she was certain of it. She knew it deep from the bottom of her heart. He loved her and wanted to marry her because of who she was, nothing more. Maisie rationalized to herself that Lauren probably had to say negative things about

Bryson because he was her brother's love rival. She was protecting family.

And it was a family that Maisie would be a part of soon enough. As soon as the wedding vows were done, she would be included by the people that Lauren protected. That was something which probably should have made her feel better, but it did not. Unfortunately, it was not a family that she wanted to be a part of.

"That man was an absolute buffoon!" Ray suddenly laughed, shocking Maisie to the core. "I cannot believe that she was going to marry him. What an absolute nightmare, Lauren."

Lauren joined in with the nasty laughter, as if Maisie was not even there. Maisie could not believe what she was hearing. She snapped around in her seat, trying to look back at the castle she was leaving behind, but it was out of sight now. A bit like the nice brother and sister duo who picked her up.

"He was not bad," Maisie shot back quietly. It was probably not the right thing to say but she needed to defend Bryson. "He was good to me while I was there. He took care of me well."

"Hmm, sure." Lauren exaggeratedly rolled her eyes. "Because he wanted your cash. Do not be fooled. You cannot think that he actually liked you for anything else, do you?"

"I was not fooled. I do not think that I could be fooled by anyone." She was shocked to have the woman who was so kind to her before now being so cold to her.

Lauren and Ray tossed their heads back and laughed

louder. It seemed like Maisie had become the butt of the jokes. She was not quite sure what had turned her around from the center of their affections to the woman that they were laughing at, but it had somehow happened and she was upset about it.

"I might not have my memories but I am not foolish," Maisie declared, but unfortunately it came out as more of a pathetic whine than anything else. She was feeling so hurt that she had turned into a child. "I know my judgements and I still believe that Bryson only had my best interests at heart."

"Pfft, sure," Lauren shot back. "If you want to believe that, then so be it."

She leaned across and whispered something into Ray's ear before the chuckling started out once more. In Maisie's eyes, they seemed a little too close for comfort. She thought as the fiancée she should have been the one sitting next to Ray, but that was not something that she would fight for. She preferred to be alone. Instead of focusing on the pair of them because they were making her feel ill, Maisie stared out of the carriage window and tried to picture what Bryson was doing right now. Probably talking to Anice and telling her that she was not coming back.

Anice would cry, June was going to be upset, Bryson was probably just angry. Angry that he had been sucked into a romance that was not real. He would not be annoyed that she was taken from him before he could take everything from her because Maisie refused to believe that. There was just no way. She did not care what Lauren and Ray thought of her for sticking by her memories of Bryson.

They could laugh at her all they wanted. She knew the truth. The truth was he was better than both of them.

They could be cold with her, but she would be cold right back.

This was not the love story that she wanted to be in.

Chapter 15

"I do not feel well." The sensation struck Maisie hard. She was not quite sure where it came from, but as it washed over her she knew that it would not be long until she vomited. "The motion of the carriage..." She slapped her hand over her mouth, no longer concerned about acting like a Lady in front of these people. "I cannot stand it. I feel like I am going to... to throw up. I do not think I can hold it in."

"Do not be so ridiculous," Lauren snapped back. "The carriage is not even moving that quickly. We are not far enough away from the castle to be stopping. Just pull yourself together, Maisie. Stop it."

Maisie nodded like this was a reasonable suggestion, like she could just stop feeling ill. She barely even took on board the harshness of Lauren's tone because the urge to be sick was so overwhelming that she could hardly breathe under the strain of it. It was causing an intense dizziness inside of her brain, a churning sensation in the pit of her stomach. There was also the issue of the small voice at the back of her head screaming at her that all of this was wrong. The further away she got, the worse it became.

"You are terribly green," Ray snarled, his face twisting up into something ugly. The sight of him like this scared Maisie in a strange, unexpected way. He kind of looked like he was a snake... the snake from her nightmares... but as much as she wanted to, she could not get caught up in that terror. "I do not like that."

"I cannot..." She wanted to defend herself, but the sensation of illness was too much.

"Urgh, she is disgusting." Ray cowered away from Maisie. "Lauren, she really is ill. I do not like it."

"We are not stopping," Lauren growled. "We need to get away from that place. I do not trust him."

There was a whole bunch of fear bursting around in Maisie's brain. She knew that all of this was not right, she was afraid by Lauren's words, but the dizziness was too much. She could not quite work everything out. Maisie leaned forwards and put her head between her knees, trying to stop the intensity of the painful butterflies flapping around in the pit of her stomach, but it did not work one bit.

Who did she not trust? Who was she trying to get Maisie away from? What was going on?

"I need to stop," Maisie insisted in the strongest voice that she could manage. It did not matter that it was barely a whisper. One of the brother sister duo had to pick up on how serious she was. "I cannot do this any longer. I need to stop, or I will end up throwing up all over the carriage, all over you."

Those words were enough to freak Ray out. He was not in the mood to have Maisie's sick all over him. He insisted that they stop the carriage so forcefully that even Lauren listened to him.

"I am not happy about this," she said over and over again, making it obvious that it was an inconvenience. "I am not happy about this at all. I do not see why we have to make this break. It causes problems for us, you know that. The sooner that we get back and deal with things, the better."

But it was too late now. The carriage had stopped and Maisie was in the process of staggering out onto the hard floor. She needed to stand on the earth, to have the solid ground underneath her, to be steady at last. She no longer cared about Lauren and her nastiness, there was a sickness inside of her that absolutely needed to get out. There was nothing that she could do to stop it.

"Do not be long," Lauren yelled out as Maisie vanished around the other side of the carriage to puke in private. "We need to get going again as soon as we can. We do not have time for this."

As Maisie bent forward and grabbed on to her knees, to finally allow the vomit to spill free from her, tears rolled down her face some more. She tried to put the crying down to not liking being sick, but that was something no one enjoyed, the tears were really related to everything that she had left behind.

Bryson. Every single time that she thought about him, the sadness washed over her in waves. She wished that she could be back with him, back in his arms, back where she needed to be. When she thought of him, she yearned to re-do everything without the shock, so she could tell Ray and Lauren that she wanted to stay with Bryson. She wept as she thought about everything she should have done. She could have told Ray that any promise she made to him before she lost her memory no longer mattered. She should have insisted that she stay with Bryson and Anice because she loved them. She loved them and felt like a part of their family more than she ever could the pair of them. They were so unwelcoming.

Eventually, Maisie felt like all of the vomit was gone, that she was done being sick, but she was not ready to step back into the carriage. She had lost the ability to care about Lauren's rant. Just because she wanted to leave at the speed of light, did not mean they had to. Maisie was allowed some fresh air before she had to sit back in the horrible atmosphere within that carriage.

She stepped away from the carriage for a while and gulped in as much air as she could, wondering what way her life should go next. This was a crossroads in her life, she had a choice right now, and she needed to make the right one. Maisie grabbed out her medallion and held it tightly between her fingers as she attempted to choose. She did not want to let her family down, she always wanted to be right by her father, but he was no longer alive. Some accident had killed him, so she could not ask him to give her permission to change her mind and who she wanted to marry. It was a decision that she needed to make herself.

I could continue to make my father proud, she told

herself. I could go along with what he wanted for me, or... well, I could chose the man who I know will love me forever more.

When she put it like that, it did not seem like a challenging choice. Of course, she should go with what she wanted because it was her life to live and she certainly wanted to be happy through it. She could also rationalize that her father would want the same for her and would say so if he were alive, but the whole idea made her nervous. Here she was, in the middle of nowhere, deciding whether or not to leave the man she had agreed to marry at a time of her life when she could not remember. Not only that, she was also going to have to deal with Ray's terrifying sister, who clearly liked things to go her way.

"This is ridiculous," Lauren shrieked at a volume where Maisie could hear her, like a terrible reminder that nothing from this point onwards would be simple. "How long does it take to vomit. Check on her, Ray. I do not care if you are averse to seeing vomit. We need to get out of here quickly."

"If I do not face them now, I shall have to listen to that screaming forever."

Maisie instinctively knew that Lauren was very involved in Ray's life. It was why they seemed so close. Clearly, she did not have a husband of her own or it would have been very unlikely that she would go out on the mission like she did. Maisie did not want to listen to Lauren's yelling forever.

"I could run away," she whispered to herself. "I could be at Goraidh Castle very quickly."

Her feet already wanted to run. She wanted to take off and just keep on running until there was nothing but dust behind her. She wanted to lose Lauren and Ray right now, forgetting about them forever more, but even in her muddled dizzy and sickly state, she knew it would not work like that. If Ray had fought so hard to find her once, then it was likely he would do so again. She needed things to be done for good this time. Maisie hardly wanted to spend the rest of her life looking over her shoulder in fear.

"I will never be free unless I speak to Ray right now," she realized. "I have to tell him that I am leaving."

She sucked in a couple of deep breaths, trying to swallow down the intense ball of fear that lodged itself in her throat. It should not have been this hard to say how she was feeling. If Ray really did love her then he would want her to be happy, even if it did not mean she was with him. However, it did not feel that way.

She stepped slowly, trying to brace herself for the awkward conversation that was to come, pausing every single time she heard Lauren screaming something else obscene about her. The screaming might have been frightening, but it merely reinforced what she needed to do. She needed to get out.

It was surely alright to break an engagement if it was not right. She was confident that her father would agree. The more that she settled on her decision, the more she decided that she was right. The tighter that she held on to her medallion, the more convinced she was that she could feel her mother's love and support. Everything was going to turn out alright. Now, she simply needed to pick her moment.

"I am sick of this whole debacle, Ray," Lauren growled, a little quieter this time around, but Maisie could still hear every single word. "I do not like pretending. It is hard to act like I do not hate her."

"I am not sure that you are acting well," Ray laughed. "I think Maisie has already worked out that you are not too fond. At least I am keeping up the pretense that we are in love. She is really falling for it."

What the hell? Maisie's blood ran ice cold as she heard those words. What was going on? Falling? For what? What were they acting about?

"Yes, well you are good at acting like a heart throb, Ray. I have always said that about you. In the past you have been too good. Do you remember how many times we almost got caught out?"

They giggled, the pair of them, and it was a strange sound. Not the sort of laugh that a brother and sister should have been sharing. But Maisie was not in her right mind, was she? She had been ill, so she could not trust her own judgements. Perhaps this was completely normal in their hometown and she had simply forgotten. She had been at Goraidh Castle for too long so assumed everything there was normal.

Well, even if life with Bryson was not the most normal, it was what she wanted, so she still needed to speak with Ray, to cancel their engagement once and for all. Maisie just wanted to wait for the right moment. She did not want to get in the middle of something weird here. This would be difficult enough.

Any minute now, she said to herself and her heart pounded wildly against her rib cage. Any minute now...

Chapter 16

"You are a bad boy, Ray." Maisie could not ignore it, the strange flirting tone in Lauren's voice. It was too weird for words. This was his sister, she herself was his fiancée. It was disgusting. And the story that they had given her had to be the truth or why else would they bother trying to find her the way they had done? "A very bad boy. I do not know what I should do with you out here in the woods."

"Just act exactly as you would if we were back in the castle," Ray purred back, somehow managing not to sound like his sister was freaking him out with her nonsense. He sounded a lot too much like a man who actually liked it. "She will be gone for a long time. I believe we have a moment."

There was a pause in the conversation, aside from some strange noises. Maisie knew that this was her moment to brave peeking around the corner to see what the hell was going on. Unfortunately, she found herself frozen to the spot, absolutely unable to do anything. Much as she wanted, no, needed to see, she was much too afraid. She knew now for certain that she should have remained with Bryson. These people were odd, even if there was a flickering of recognition within her, it was not enough. They were strangers to her, and she did not like them. She did not want to be with them any longer.

"I do not think that I can undress you rapidly here," Ray suddenly declared, sounding much too disappointed. "I would love to see that naked flesh of yours, but this is not the place."

"It might not be the place for that," Lauren shot back. "But there are plenty of other things that we can do here. I mean, take a look around. I might not have wanted to stop here initially, but actually little miss forget the world might have a good point. It is a nice empty clearing in a woodland, but far enough from anywhere, so that we will not be disturbed. I even believe that we can hide whatever we need to."

What would they need to hide? None of them really had anything with them. Not that Maisie was aware of, anyway. But then again, it seemed like she did not know anything that was happening around her.

"Ooh, I do like it when you whisper into my ear," Ray chuckled loudly. "Tell me more."

Maisie felt like she needed to lean forward quickly, to find out what was going on before the whole world imploded around her. She was on the edge already, it seemed like she was on the verge of losing her damn mind, so there was nothing left to hold her back. She needed to overcome her fear and just see. So, she edged herself, slowly, trying not to make any sort of sound. Maisie knew she could not be seen...

"Oh, my goodness." But any need to be sensible and smart simply floated away the moment she spotted what was really going on between Lauren and Ray. Much as she had suspected it, it was another level of horror to see it happening before her very eyes. Brother and sister were kissing, kissing like there was no tomorrow, kissing with a similar passion to what she shared with Bryson...

Maisie clapped her hands to her mouth with shock. This was too much for her. She could not marry a man who spent time kissing his sister, that was horrible. There was no way that her father would want her to get mixed up in a family like that. He could not have known what was going on with these two...

Unless... all of a sudden, the fog cleared from her brain and she began to realize just how stupid she had been. They were obviously not brother and sister, or family at all. Bryson had asked for proof that they knew Maisie, but he did not think to enquire their family link. And why would he? Unless he thought that they were tricking her. Clearly, that was exactly what they were doing. They wanted all of that money and land her father had before he passed away. Everything that Lauren had informed her Bryson wanted from her, it was actually the pair of them. Ray would marry her and then they would have it all.

"You want to do that here?" Maisie snapped back into her hiding position as the kissing broke apart and Ray began asking questions to Lauren which Maisie did not understand. "I suppose..."

"It is perfect, if you think about it," Lauren replied. "And we are going to have to do it fast. Who knows what memories you sparked by mentioning the silly girl's parent's names in front of her?"

Maisie sucked in and held a breath, now more terrified than she had ever been before. Ray discussing her parents had not shaken a lot, but she did get a feeling then that he was being honest with her.

"I had to discuss her parents. We needed Bryson to believe us, did we not?"

"And what exactly would you have done if she recalled everything there and then? How could we have gotten out of that mess? I will admit that your risky strategy did pay off, but it was a scary moment."

"So, because of that, we need to put our plan into action right away? That is what you think, Lauren?"

Maisie's fingers curled around the waist of her wedding dress simply because she needed something to grip on to, to remind her that this was in fact real and not some horrible nightmare that she was caught in the middle of. There really was something horrible going on here, and unfortunately, she needed to work out what. She no longer needed to explain to Ray why she was leaving, he was not the nice fiancé that she first assumed he might be, but this was her past and she needed some truth.

"We cannot allow her to regain her memories, Ray, you know that as well as I do. The closer that we get to home, the more chance there is of her remembering everything. We came to get her to make sure that she does not recall who she really is or that would ruin everything for us, so why not here?"

"Why not here?" Ray repeated, with little to no hesitation in his tone. "I suppose you are right."

"You need to seduce her, you know, Ray," Lauren declared with a teasing to her tone. Maisie's stomach churned. There was no way in hell that she would allow Ray anywhere near her, much less seduce her. "And when you get her far enough away from here to somewhere you can hide her, you must stab her."

Maisie let out an audible gasp of shock. She clamped her lips shut tightly, praying that no one had heard her, and thankfully, it seemed immediately like no one was coming after her. Lauren and Ray must have been so wrapped in one another that they did not notice her. Thank goodness.

They were planning to kill her... of course they were. Now that she had heard it coming from their mouths, it was utterly obvious that was what they wanted to do with her. Although Maisie could not understand why they wanted her dead now. Surely, it would work out better for them to get Ray married off to her first. They would not be able to access anything without her, they would be entitled to nothing.

"I have to be the one who kills her?" Ray moaned. "But why does it have to be me? You are so much better at it. You have the stomach for it, my love. Since you have killed before."

Maisie's head spun wildly under this brand new, very unpleasant knowledge. She was with killers, people who did not care who they got rid of to get to where they wanted to be, so she stood very little chance. If they decided to come at her, she would be killed where no one could hear her scream.

"But I know how much you hate Maisie, and all of Ferguson family, so the honor is yours."

"I do hate them with an intense passion," Ray agreed, much to Maisie's dismay. What could she have possibly done to deserve such a visceral reaction? "But I do not need to be the one to kill her."

"I have had enough killing." Lauren sounded a little angrier now. Maisie could tell that she was growing increasingly frustrated with Ray. What Maisie did not understand was why she had not run yet. "I have had plenty of killing in my lifetime. You think that it was easy to murder my husband?"

"I think that you found it very easy to kill Duncan Ferguson." The name made Maisie freeze. That name was all too familiar. It was the name given to her by Ray, the name of her father. Lauren was married to him? She was... was her stepmother? That made Ray... well, Lauren's lover, she assumed. And they killed her father and now wanted her dead as well. Her mother must have died a long time ago...

Which means there was no accident. Not for her father at any rate. That could explain why Maisie remembered her father and not her mother. Lauren was not Ray's sister, Lauren was a cold-blooded killer and she needed Maisie dead before her memories came back so... oh God, so that she could claim Maisie's father's estate. She did have a claim to everything after all. And Maisie was the only thing standing in her way. The faster that Maisie put the puzzle pieces back together, the more she feared.

Her life was in danger, that much was the truth. She really needed to get away.

"You killed that old bastard like he meant nothing to you," Ray continued with a little laugh as if this was all just a joke and not related to someone's life at all. "You were coldhearted, Lauren, just as I love you, and I think that you could be just as coldhearted with that bitch as well. I believe in you."

"I am not killing her, Ray," Lauren insisted, like they were arguing over a pack of cards or something. "You are going to kill her because we both need to commit murder. That is the only way I can be sure that we are in it together. So, you are going to take this dagger and get rid of your little wife, now."

"And if she is found?" Ray shot back instantly. "Who can we blame it on this time?"

"I don't care. Bryson, maybe. Why the hell not? That guy was weird anyway. If Maisie's body is ever found, which will not happen because you are going to do a good job, then we can blame it on him. We are good at passing off murder on someone else, do you not think? We did a good job with Duncan."

"Maisie helped us with that because she ran away as soon as she realized that you were pinning it up on her, but Bryson will have a whole clan of people who know otherwise..."

"A clan that live nowhere near us, Ray, so stop making excuses, will you. Just get out there and kill her. You cannot get away with this. You have to do it. Right here, right now."

Something was happening to Maisie, something was stirring deep within her. She could not explain it, but she could not move as it happened. She did not know much, but she was aware that she had to wait where she was while it washed over her, sinking into her fully.

Chapter 17

"Murder?" All of a sudden, something hit Maisie hard. "You killed him. Ray saw you with a bloody knife.

She could hardly breathe as this horrible memory overcame her. It was the first full memory that she had experienced ever since she lost her whole life, and it was a bad one. It was Lauren and Ray sneering over her, yelling at her, and letting her know that they were going to pin her father's murder on her.

"Oh, my God," she whispered to herself with her hand clutched to her chest as her foolishness hit her hard. How could she not remember that from the very first second she laid eyes on Lauren?

This woman was her wicked stepmother. She knew that she was evil instantly but did not feel like she could say anything because it was the first time that her father had found happiness. Her mother died in childbirth, that was why she did not know her. So, when he fell in love with

Lauren, she could do nothing. Even when she suspected that Lauren only wanted her father's money. Did she suspect murder though?

Her head hurt. It ached a lot, so much that Maisie knew it would be a challenge to move, but she no longer had any choice in the matter. Lauren murdered her father and would see her dead too. She was not sure who would end up being the one who put the knife into her, but it hardly mattered.

She gripped on to the medallion hard, allowing some tears to trickle down her cheeks. She had been holding on to the dream that she would get to see her mother again, that she would be the one to explain who she was, but that would no longer be possible. Her mother had never been alive at the same time as her, and now her father had been taken away as well. All that Maisie could do was cry for them.

"Bryson," she whispered to herself as she finally managed to stagger away from the carriage, breaking the power that it had over her at long last. "I want Bryson. I just want to be with him."

That was where she would head now. She did not know the direction in which she needed to head, but somehow she would find it, she would find him once more. Maisie could only hope that Bryson would still want her after everything that she had put him through. Especially now that she knew some of the truth.

"I will go back the way that we came," she hissed to herself. "At least, what I think anyway. That will be the best way. Back the way that I came and somehow... somehow I will find him once more."

Every step pulled her away from Lauren and Ray, away from the impending doom in which they threatened her with, but it was not enough. Nothing was ever going to be enough. This would scare her, as would the memories that Lauren had brought back to her. No wonder she blocked everything out. Her past life was so unpleasant, something that she absolutely needed to escape from.

"They want me dead and buried," she whispered to herself as she wiped away some of the tears soaking her face. "So that they can have a fortune that I do not even want. Even if it does belong to me."

Maisie could not see that her life was worth any amount of money. Or anyone's life for that matter, but there were clearly greedy people in the world who did not see it that way. These were the sort of people that she wanted to spend the rest of her life avoiding. They were horrid, she just wished that her father had seen it. Maisie could not understand how she had allowed herself to be tricked by the idea that her father wanted her to marry Ray. He would never want her anywhere near that pig. Not a chance.

"Keep going," she hissed as she stepped backwards, trying to tip toe so as not to draw any attention to herself. "Keep going until you can start running and never look back. Keep going, do this..."

As soon as Maisie picked up the pace, she would make noise, and she was going to have to outrun the pair of them. It was not going to be easy which was why she needed to get a head start on them. Right now, Ray and Lauren were arguing over what action they were going to take next, who was going to murder her, which was why she needed to take full advantage of this freedom while she still had it.

Snap. Maisie jumped. She did not know what twig caused the snapping sound, but she was pretty sure that it was loud enough for Ray and Lauren to hear, which meant that it was time to go. No more freaking out and being quiet. She would have to use every scrap of strength within her to make it back to Bryson.

I am coming for you, Bryson, she thought desperately as she took off at the speed of light. I am, I promise. We are going to have the wedding that we want, the live that we need, the happy ever after at last.

Of course, she could not be certain that would all happen, right now it was only a dream, but it was better than focusing in on the nightmare that she was currently existing in. The nightmare that had been haunting her for as long as she had been with Bryson. The snake coming for her, trying to kill her.

The snake was Lauren and Ray. It was always Lauren and Ray, she just did not realize it before. They had always been coming for her, nipping at her heels, wanting to take her down and crush her dead.

Her head pounded, her legs ached, but she did not stop. She kept on running, even when it became difficult in the wedding dress, even as the wedding dress caught on a nearby branch and tore. There was a part of Maisie that simply wanted to whip the dress off and throw it to the floor to make it easier for her to run, but she did not have the time to pause for even a second. That would take too long. Anything would.

"Argh!" She stumbled, she tumbled forwards. Her hands slapped onto the floor hard. She cried out in agony, pretty sure that she would have blood there now. On her hands and maybe even leaving a trail behind her. Anything that could leave a trail for them to find her was bad news. "Argh, oh, my God."

She tried to get herself upwards once more, but her dress made it challenging. She continued to fall over and over again, which only brought about more tears. She was a mess, a real mess, which was not helping her one bit. Maisie knew that she needed to suck in some more air if she was going to calm down, but that felt impossible. She could not get any air into her lungs however hard she tried.

"Come... come on, Maisie," she hissed to herself. "Come on. You need to get to Bryson."

She thought of Bryson, only Bryson as she rose to her feet. His memory got her moving once more. She remembered all of their special moments together, every kiss that they had shared, every special night. It helped her, it made her feel better, it made her freer... so free that other memories returned to her as well. Memories from her previous life. Playing with her father, him giving her his undivided attention, laughing and giggling as she raced around the castle, her castle, her thinking that her life was always going to be safe with her father. How little she knew about what was eventually going to come her way.

She knew her life now though and that was a good thing. Those memories were a part of her, she could own them, even the ones involving Lauren which she did not like so much. If she could claim them for her own then she could start moving forward with her life properly, if she could escape these people.

Maisie felt exactly the same as she did in her nightmares as she was trying to escape the snake that was coming for her. Every step was just as painful, the ice-cold fear hurt her just as much, it was as if her body had been trying to prepare her for this exact moment the entire time. Her nightmares were premonitions, warnings of what was about to come. She should have paid more attention.

"Bryson!" Maisie called out loudly, the moment she felt like it was all getting too much for her, that the exhaustion was really beginning to weigh her down. "Bryson, please come for me. I need you."

He was her hero once before, he saved her by the river when she was getting away from Lauren, Ray, and the accusation of murder, so maybe he could do it again. Fate had brought them together as he happened to stumble across her while he was out for a horse ride. Maybe the same could occur again.

"Bryson, come for me," she wailed, her sadness aching her lungs just as much as the running now. "I cannot do this much longer. I am afraid that I will end up dying because I am tired..."

She staggered and tripped forwards again, knowing that if she fell once more, she would not get back up. She did not have the strength to keep on going. Perhaps it was better for her to find a hiding place until Lauren and Ray gave up on her. Surely there had to come a time when they would assume that they could not catch up with her and they would let her go... or was that a pipe dream? If they had succeeded in following her to Bryson's castle and the wedding, then there was a chance they would never give up.

Eventually, Maisie found a rock big enough to hide herself behind. She tucked herself out of sight and sucked in plenty of air in the hope that she would finally return to normal. She needed to get her breathing under control, or her panting and rasping would make it so much easier for them to find her.

"Calm down," she whispered. "Calm down and hold on to the medallion. It has always helped you."

Maisie held on to the medallion with her shaking hands, trying her hardest to hold it together while the whole world around her was falling apart. The medallion was the only thing that had helped her through the time when she did not know who she was. Someone had tried to steal it from her and got everything else, but the medallion... oh, which could have been what happened to her in the first place.

Wow, someone had tried to steal from her, someone had hurt her, and she still managed to keep the medallion. Even when she had been so badly injured that she lost her memories, she kept it with her. And certainly not because Ray had given it to her, but because it was the only thing that she had of her mother.

The medallion had saved her before, and it would do so again. All Maisie needed to do was cling on to the medallion and keep it with her at all times. Without the medallion, she could not go on existing in the world, and that was all she wanted. But she did not need to worry about that. She had the medallion and her mother protecting her. She was going to be fine. She had to be. It was the only way that she would ever see Bryson again.

Chapter 18

"What the hell was that?" Ray snapped angrily. Much as Lauren had started to grow impatient with him, he was becoming increasingly irritated by her as well. He had simply assumed that she would do the killing since she seemed to enjoy it so much last time. He did not really care enough about Maisie either way to do the dreaded deed. Really, all that he wanted was to have her gone so that he could get his spoils at long last. He was not necessarily with Lauren for her sparkling personality, but for what she could offer him.

"What are you moaning about now?" Lauren snapped back. "I do not want to hear any more of your excuses. This is just getting silly now, Ray. I could not be more annoyed with you if I tried..."

"This is no excuse." He pushed away from her, no longer desiring Lauren's hot body. He had something else more important in mind. "I heard something. Surely, it is taking far too long for Maisie to be sick. I think that something has happened. I believe the girl might be running away."

A stream of unpleasant curse words flew out of Lauren's mouth as she ran to the other side of the carriage to see if Ray was right. If the girl had run off while they were arguing, then she was going to be so damn annoyed. If Ray would just do what she told him to without causing any issues, then they would not be in this position. Sure enough, there was a disgusting pile of vomit by Lauren's feet, but no one attached to it. An intense rage so powerful she feared she might erupt like a volcano overtook her.

"Ray, look what you have done!" she screamed. "You have put off the killing for so long she has gone."

"I did nothing wrong." Ray was behind Lauren in a heartbeat. "I do not know what you are talking about."

"I bet it is because you mentioned her parent's names." Lauren flung her elbow backwards so it would dig into Ray's ribs. Instantly he doubled forwards in pain. "I bet her memories returned..."

"If I had not said anything then she would not have been allowed to come with us."

"I am the one who spoke out about the medallion. You cannot take credit for that."

"No, but for some reason you think that it is alright to blame me for her running away, Lauren. You know, I get sick of this sometimes." Ray threw his hands in the air in frustration. "I am like your lap dog. Always the one there just so you do not have to take responsibility for yourself. You always choose me to be the fall guy. That is why I have had to sit back and wait while you always do what you want."

"What do you mean?" Lauren's intense fury was growing by the moment. "I have done nothing..."

"I had to sit back and wait while you married that old man, showing him affection in front of me..."

"You think I wanted that?" Lauren screamed. "You think that was fun for me? It was dreadful. I believe that I am the only one who has sacrificed for us here. For some reason, you cannot see that."

"I do not know why you are acting like this, Lauren. I have sacrificed as well," Ray insisted.

"Not as much as me." Lauren's hands flew on to her hips in defiance. "You will not even kill the girl."

"No one will kill her if we cannot find her," he growled right back. "She has vanished. She might be running back to Bryson right now to tell him what we were planning for her. Perhaps she even overheard us talking. You are not exactly known for your quiet voice, are you?" Lauren snorted but chose not to respond to that one. "If Maisie does have her memories back and she is going to tell him, then not only will a war start between our clans, but we will be outed. Not everyone will believe her, but some might."

As irritated as she was, Lauren understood what Ray was saying. Maisie running off was problematic for the pair of them. They absolutely had to catch her and kill her before she revealed anything.

"We must split up," Lauren insisted. "She will have run off that way, away from us, out of our sight, and back the way that she came. Especially if she is looking for Bryson. I have my sgian dubh with me." Lauren pulled out her Scottish dagger from her pocket. "Do you have any weapons? Just in case."

"I do." Ray nodded determinedly. "I have my sword with me. So, I guess whoever finds her first will be the one to do the deed. As long as it is done, then me and you are safe. And that is the main thing."

Finally, on the same page at long last, Ray and Lauren nodded determinedly at one another. It was time to head out into the woods as quickly as they could manage, to finish off the plan that they started all those months ago when Duncan Ferguson met his end. He was supposed to be the only one who died. His daughter was going to take the blame and spend her life in jail, with Lauren telling the sad story of jealousy and grief sending her crazy, but since things had changed, this was how it would end up panning out.

"Let us get going then," he declared. "I shall take this path and you take the other. We can meet back here once the deed is done and continue on building the life together that we have been working on."

Lauren was glad to have Ray back on her side at long last. They needed to work together to ensure this all worked, and they came out on top, so this was good. And Ray might have to kill after all. Lauren really needed him to kill. It was the only way that she would be able to truly respect him as a man and believe that he was on the same page as her. Right now, she was not sure if she needed to get rid of him too…

Every noise made Maisie jump. She was not sure if she was being chased or not, she did not know if Lauren and Ray could find her where she was hiding, but she continued to freak out more and more with every second that passed. She had needed the break because running was getting too much for her, but as her body finally calmed down, she was not sure that she should have stopped after all. Maisie did not know if she would ever be able to move from this position again. She feared any movement would lead to her discovery and she had no idea how long Ray and Lauren would keep looking for her.

I cannot stay here forever, she tried to tell herself desperately. Otherwise I will die anyway.

Maisie did not want to be killed by the people who were determined to wipe out her family for financial gain, but she also preferred not to freeze or starve to death. At some point, she was going to have to recover from the throbbing inside of her body to continue on with her journey to Bryson.

Get yourself together, her brain hissed at her. It is time to move in a moment. You have to.

She experimented with trying to get her legs shifting, just a little bit, but it was as if they had been encased in lead. They did not want to go anywhere because she felt much safer where she was.

"It has gone quiet," Maisie whispered to herself, needing to break the odd silence. "It is time to go."

She counted herself down from ten, trying to prepare herself for what was to come, before she finally did the unthinkable and she dragged herself upwards. She pulled herself to her feet and allowed her eyes to dart anxiously around. Thank goodness there was no one. Not a soul looking back at her, not even a bird. Maisie allowed a small smile to play on her lips as she thought of herself as foolish. How could she be so silly? Lauren and Ray were probably still entangled in one another. They did not hear her fall at all. And even if they had done, clearly they were not bothered enough to follow her. She was free to leave and walk at whatever pace she wanted to. She did want to be fast though, but that was because she missed Bryson so much. Maisie needed to come back with him sooner rather than later. She could hardly stand this...

"There you are you little bitch!" The words rocketed through Maisie so painfully that she almost fell once more. Lauren seemed to appear as if from nowhere and she had taken on the true appearance of a mad woman. Her hair was all over the place, her face filled with sheer fury, her clothing all covered in mud and sticks from the forest. Not that Maisie thought she looked much better herself, and even worse she was wearing a wedding dress. "You thought that you could escape me, and your fate?"

The sgian dubh waved in the air and Maisie immediately knew that it was meant for her. She tried to run off once more, but Lauren had taken on an inhuman amount of strength and she pounced on Maisie, knocking her to the ground. Pain seemed to come from every angle, Maisie could not keep her thoughts straight. She was doing her best to bat away Lauren's hands as they came for her over and over again, to punch and stab her, but it was impossible. Lauren's rage and greed transformed her into something else.

"I have... wanted you dead... every moment since I met you," Lauren puffed out in between every attack. "I hate you, Maisie... Ferguson. You are... pathetic. An absolute... waste of life. I hate you so much."

The viciousness in Lauren's words was only overtaken by her attacks. Maisie knew that this was a life and death situation, so her main focus needed to be on the blade. If the sgian dubh got to her, then everything would be over. If she could knock that from Lauren's hand then she would stand a chance.

"Oh, my goodness, stop fighting back, Maisie," Lauren spat out. "Accept your fate already."

And there it was. The blade hanging over her head, aiming for her heart. It was now or never. Lauren had the expression of someone who already thought that she had won, which was not good news for Maisie. If she was going to keep herself alive then this was the moment that she needed to act.

Maisie reached up. She grabbed the blade between her fingers and twisted it around. She could feel it cutting into her skin and piercing her but it was better that her hand get injured than her body. She did her best to block out the sheer agony and used as much force as she could manage, she tuned out everything that was going on inside of her body, she focused only on her mind because that was what would get her thought and keep her alive. It was not easy against Lauren, who had rage on her side, but Maisie thought of Bryson, of June and Anice, of everyone that she wanted to keep herself living for. She thought of them and fought for them as well, twisting Lauren's wrist around until the woman howled and loosened her grip. Maisie was not expecting it, but thoughts of the life that she really wanted gave her strength and finally she was the one holding the sgian dubh.

Chapter 19

"Get off me," Maisie panted. She turned the sgian dubh around to show Lauren. Not to threaten her, but just to make her move. "I am not going to let you kill me, Lauren. You will not get what you want to. You want money and my father's estate? Fine, that is not worth my life. You can have it. You do not deserve it, especially since you were the one who killed my father, but I will not die for it as well."

Lauren raised herself up so that she could stare at Maisie, but she did not get off. She was not done murdering Maisie yet. She did not care what the girl said, she was going to finish her off.

"I do not trust you, Maisie Ferguson," Lauren sneered. "You are untrustworthy. All people born in your position are. You do not know about hardships and real life. You have no idea how someone like me has to fight to get to the top. All that will happen if I let you go is that you will run back to your boyfriend and tell him everything. Bryson will then rage war on me and Ray, and we will never be allowed to live in peace."

"I will not say anything." Maisie knew that deep down she was probably not being honest with Lauren, but she would have said anything in that moment to put an end to the nightmare that she was living in. In all of the dreams that she had suffered leading up to this moment, she had never been caught. This was something new to her and she was not quite sure how to negotiate it properly. "I will simply tell Bryson that I only want to be with him, so I ended the engagement with Ray. You will never hear from me again. I will even take on the name Rosalyn because that is what I have been living with anyway."

Lauren tossed her head back and laughed nastily. "This is how I know that you are a liar, Maisie. Stop trying to pretend that you are a much better person than I am. Stop acting like you are above us all. We are all terrible people. At least I am honest enough to admit who I am. You are not an angel."

That word shocked Maisie to the core. She assumed that Lauren did not know how Bryson referred to her and this was just a coincidence, but still she froze exactly as she was with the blade pointed upwards and Lauren staring at her with sheer hatred in her eyes. She wanted to be an angel, she wanted to be a good person, she did not understand what Lauren meant about everyone being evil...

"Oh, for goodness sake, I am not tolerating this any longer." Lauren pulled an arm back to snatch the blade from Maisie. "You are going to die here on the forest floor and be forgotten by everyone..."

But something happened. Lauren seemed to misjudge her own weight. She could not hold herself up with one arm like she thought that she was going to be able to and she fell. She tumbled, screaming, onto Maisie, her full weight squashing the girl. Maisie let out a strangled sound of pain and yelled for Lauren to get off of her, but she did not seem to be moving. It was as if she wanted to choke the air from Maisie and finish her off that way. A much slower murder than a stab wound, but probably effective.

"Why am I all wet?" Maisie blurted out. "There is a warm wetness. What is happening?"

She used every scrap of strength left within her to shove Lauren to the side. It was a little shocking that Lauren was not fighting back after her determination to have Maisie killed, but that was something she simply decided to be grateful for. Lauren hit the forest floor and Maisie sucked in more air than she had ever needed before, trying to regain the wind that had been stripped from her lungs.

"What is this?" The warm wetness remained upon her. Maisie patted her hands over herself and screamed as her hands were covered in red. Blood, it had to be, but where was she bleeding from? She could not feel any stab wounds, but since she had never been stabbed before, she did not know what it should feel like. Perhaps she needed a moment for the shock to wear off and then it would come to her.

"I am covered in blood." Maisie tried to wash it off of herself, but it covered too much of it. It had sunk into the fabric. It did not seem like there was anything that she could do about it. "Oh no, this is bad..."

If this was the end of her life, then she wanted it to be filled with happy memories. She wanted to think of Bryson and everything that he had done for her. She needed to recall what it felt like to be loved. Yet somehow, he would not come to her. It was as if something was blocking his path and he could not get to her. There was still something that she needed to figure out before she could cave to her injuries.

"Oh, no." Panic set in. Maisie instantly scooted away from Lauren. She tried desperately to figure out what was going on here. She did not know fully what was happening and it had her panicked. "Lauren."

Lauren lay beside her, motionless, with a glassy stare to her eyes. Her gaze was fixed on nothing yet pointed up towards the sky like she was waiting for something to come to her there. Maisie could not accept the sight of the sgian dubh sticking up from her chest, piercing her heart, clearly killing her instantly.

"I am a murderer," Maisie realized. It did not matter that Lauren had fallen onto the dagger, the end result was the same. "I pointed the sgian dubh at her, I threatened her with it, and now she is dead."

She leaned to the left-hand side and tried to throw up once more to let some of her negative feelings out, but Maisie had nothing left inside of her. Nothing but a bitter burning bile which made her sicker.

"I have killed," she wept. "I am as bad as them. I am no better than Lauren and Ray... oh, no."

As soon as she recalled Ray's existence something snapped inside of Maisie. She leapt up and began running, her animalistic survival instinct setting in. She could not be next to Lauren's body when Ray finally came across her, then she really would die. Maisie felt awful, knowing that she was running towards Bryson with even more baggage than before, but she knew him to be a wonderful man. He would care for her. He would assist her during her darkest moment because he loved her.

As Maisie ran, memories that had evaded her before flooded her and made her feel terrible. Now she could remember fully what a wonderful man her father was, and she hated Lauren for ruining him and the lovely life that they had. It hardly seemed fair for her to be destroyed as she was because of that woman. And now she had managed to wreck things again because she had turned Maisie into a killer.

"I want to be good," she cried out to herself as she ran. "That is all I have ever wanted."

Well, that and the man she was supposed to marry. She wished that she had gone through with that as well. If she had simply told Lauren and Ray that she did not wish to go with them then no one would have had to die. If they had asked her about her father's fortune, she would have told them to take it. She had love, she did not need anything from her father as well. Certainly not if they wanted her dead.

"I did not want my father to die," she howled as the tears began to make it challenging for her to see. "I did not want anyone to lose their life. I just wanted to have a normal life."

The medallion was still between her fingers, reminding

her of her mother, but this was not enough to comfort her any longer. Maisie no longer felt like someone who deserved her mother's love and comfort because she was so bad, rotten to the core. Her mother would never support her becoming a killer.

The next time that Maisie stumbled she allowed herself to fall to the ground willingly. She no longer had the fight within her to keep on going. If Ray was going to find her and kill her then so be it. It was all that she deserved anyway. Maisie could not live with herself, knowing that she was a murderer.

"Just find me," she whimpered into the dirt. "Find me and end me. I am bad as well. I deserve nothing."

She could not hear anything other than her own weeping for a while, but soon footsteps rocketed behind her. Maisie ignored the animal instinct inside of her that wanted to run because it would not get her anywhere anyway. She had no choice but to lie where she was and wait for death to come for her.

"It is happening." She braced herself right at the moment a giant weight leapt on her and caused her head to smack on the floor hard. Maisie's headache became ten times worse but that was the least of her problems right now. "It is happening, and I do not get to say goodbye to Bryson. That is all I regret."

"Where is Lauren?" Ray grabbed a handful of her hair and pulled it hard. "What did you do with her? She came this way to find you, yet I cannot see her. What did you do to her? Did you force her to get lost?"

"I... I..." He did not know that Lauren was dead, and

Maisie could not find the strength to tell him. She was out of her mind with the pain and the shock. She just wanted death to come for her already. She knew that Bryson was much less keen on killing than Lauren, but she did not have the patience for him to work up to it. "I do not know," Maisie stammered out. "I have not... not seen anyone..."

Ray repaid her lies by slamming her face back into the dirt. Maisie swallowed more than she ever wanted to, which caused her to cough repeatedly, trying to get the dust out of her before her lungs got infected... not that it mattered really, she would not be breathing for too much longer.

"I will kill you," Ray screamed. "I have to kill you. Lauren has ordered me to do so. She needs you dead so that she can have everything that the world believes should be yours. She wants me to kill you, but there is no point if I do not know where she is. See, for me to win in the plan, she has to be there. So, Maisie, I need you to tell me where she is and what you have done with her. It might save your life."

Maisie wanted to tell him now that Lauren was dead because it could have stripped the fight from him, but he kept hitting her head on the floor too hard. She could not find the words. Any minute now she was going to die throw the blows to the head anyway, so none of this would matter.

I am going to die, she thought to herself as the sadness crushed her painfully. I am going to die right here and my last act on earth will be killing another human...

Chapter 20

What on earth was happening? Maisie was not sure how much longer she could continue bracing herself for. This was getting silly now, why was Ray not just killing her? Was this some sort of torment?

"Fine," Maisie muttered out. "I killed her. Is that what you want to hear? That I killed Lauren? But I did not want that to happen. She was attacking me, she would not stop... I took the blade from her and I do not know what happened. I have no explanation, so just kill me already, will you? Kill me dead. It's what I deserve."

But nothing happened. Nothing at all. Maisie was starting to grow impatient with the whole situation. If Ray was no longer going to kill her then she wanted him off of her. The more that he weighed up on her, the more uncomfortable she became. She hated the feel of his body on top of hers.

"Ray?" She twisted uncomfortably but he did not

move. There seemed to be something else grabbing his attention which Maisie clocked on to not long after. A weird whistling sound that she could not place at all. "Ray, what the hell is going on? Can you please...?" She twisted over onto her back. "Get off me?"

And he did. Surprisingly, he did exactly what Maisie commanded him. Only he did not move like a normal person. He sort of slumped to one side and fell off of her, a little like Lauren did when she fell, when she was dead. But there was no sgian dubh this time, Maisie had no weapon to defend herself with. She could not be a murderer a second time around. It was far too painful for her.

"Ray, what happened?" Maisie turned to look at him, but he had fallen away from her. His body was not facing her anymore and she was far too afraid to lean closer to him, to see what had really happened. "Oh, no." She leaned forwards, with her head in her hands and wept hard. "No, no, no, no more."

It was too late to fight. Too late to run. Maisie was not sure that she could go anywhere right now. Every emotion that she could possibly feel darted through her, shocking her, sending lightning bolts all the way through her. She could not grasp on to anything. Maisie was overwhelmed by her emotions.

She seemed to be free now, free of anyone coming for her, and she had her identity back as well, which she did not expect to happen, and yet she had never felt so lost either. She wept for everything that she could have had and everything that was not going to happen anymore. She had lost.

"Ray, I... I did not mean for you to die too," she called

out. "You were not the one who killed my father. You probably did not want to kill me either. You were just doing what Lauren told you to."

She leaned forwards and held on to her knees, sobbing hard and fast. A pair of arms circled around her which she assumed to belong to Ray who was finally going to put her out of her misery. She did not fight it, she went with him as he lifted her from the floor, and she began to realize that her brain was playing tricks on her. She was attaching who she really wanted to see to the man who was going to kill her.

Bryson. The arms felt like him, the man smelt like him, at least she was feeling like she was with someone that she loved before she passed away. That was better than knowing Ray was wrapped around her. She lost herself in the daydream of Bryson, wondering how incredible her life would be if she was with him right now. She would have loved nothing more than to be in his arms, loving him.

"Bryson," she whispered to herself. "Bryson, I wish that it was you here. I wish that it was you…"

She leaned into the man's chest, inhaling him deeply, loving every second of the fantasy that she had created for herself. It did not need to be real, it could be whatever she needed it to be, and this was him. Bryson MacGregor, the only person who she had been in love with for her whole life.

"I am here." The whisper back sounded all too real, and it really did seem to be coming from Bryson as well. Her imagination was incredible. She could not believe how wonderful it was. "I am here for you."

A finger slowly wiped the tears away from her cheeks. She could not believe that this was Ray being so tender with her. He was never that sort of person. She assumed that this was imagination as well. She was creating a whole scene for herself. Or maybe she had actually died, and she was able to live in her favorite memories of all time. She wanted that. If this was what death looked like, then Maisie was alright with it.

"Oh, Bryson." She cuddled into him tighter. "I never should have left you. I never should have believed those people. It has only ever been you for me. I wish that I had stayed and married you. That is what I wanted. I was just... just afraid. I was scared. I was silly. But now I get to live in the afterlife with you. I can really be your angel. I can really be the person that you thought I was. I can be your Rosalyn."

"You are whoever you want to be," he murmured back quietly. "I will love you whoever you are. I have always loved you and I will always love you. I never should have let you go either. I love you."

She smiled to herself as her eyes began to close. This was heaven for her, it was absolutely perfect. If it had been real and Bryson had rushed to her rescue like the hero he always was for her, then it would have been the best day of her whole life. She would have loved it more than anything in the world.

"Let me see you, Maisie," Bryson whispered to her. "I need to see you. To know that you are alright."

She leaned back, knowing that it was not Bryson she was going to see, but Ray... yet her mind created him. The man smiling back at her with sheer love in his eyes was the only person she wanted to see. Maisie was grateful for that. She needed to see him, he was everything to her...

"I am here with you," she whispered quietly, reaching out to touch the gentle skin on his cheek. "I am here with the most wonderful man in the world and that is all I have ever wanted."

"I can take you back to Goraidh Castle, if that is what you want." Bryson asked her cautiously. "I know that you have another home, so I will take you there if you wish. Or I can take you with me."

"I only want to be with you. It is the only place in the world for me. Goraidh Castle all the way."

"I should not have allowed this to happen to you," Bryson told her sadly. "I wish that I had not let you go. I do apologize. It was only after you left that I recalled your nightmares, and I knew then that these were the people who had been coming for you in your dreams. These were the ones that you were having nightmares about all along. I struggled to explain that to my men, they did not understand why I would allow you to leave and then chase after you, but I was right. All along. I knew it. I could feel it."

Maisie slid her eyes closed and allowed herself to drift off into her fantasy for a little while longer. She did not want Bryson to vanish, she wanted to have him here with her for as long as she could. She was very afraid that any minute now he could vanish and there was nothing that she could do about it.

"Bryson, you had no choice," she whispered. "I was the one who was silly enough to believe in what those horrible people told me. I should have listened to my gut and known. They were not looking for me because they wanted to take care of me. It was because they wanted me dead." She chuckled mirthlessly to herself. "Lauren tried to tell me that you were the one after my father's fortune, but I knew that it was not the truth. I knew that you were not like that. You would never do anything like that. It was them. They were the ones who wanted to take from me. They wanted it all and needed me dead."

"You are not going to die," Bryson reassured her. "I have you now. There is no chance of death."

"But I am already dead," she murmured back. "I must be, or I would not be with you. You are back at Goraidh Castle, mourning because our wedding day was an absolute disaster."

"Maisie, I am here." Bryson narrowed his eyes at her, wondering why she had not picked up on that yet. "I am here with you. I came after you. I came to save you. I came to take you back from those people because I knew that I could not trust them. I knew that I should not have let you go, Maisie. Especially because I love you as much as I do. I love you and I want you with me at all times. June does too, as do the rest of the clan. And Anice... Anice misses you like crazy. She was mad at me for letting you go."

Maisie reached out and stroked his cheeks, this time accepting the strange and bizarre truth, that Bryson really was here with her. She was not his angel, not in the literal sense anyway, but he was her hero. Instinctively, Bryson had known that she needed him, and he came for her, just like he always would do.

"You are here," she cried out, weeping hard. "You are here to help me. I cannot believe how lucky I am. I cannot believe that you have come for me. I do not know how I can thank you enough..."

"You do not need to thank me," he declared back, starting to get a little emotional now as he saw the state that Maisie was working herself into. Clearly, this whole experience had been even more traumatic for her than he dared to believe. Guilt flooded him, he knew that he should not have allowed this to happen. Maisie was his fiancée and he let her walk off into danger. What sort of man did that turn him into? "I would do anything for you, Maisie. I want to always be the man to save you. I never want to be away from you again. It has been absolute torture for me, I will admit that to you now."

"I have not enjoyed it either," Maisie giggled. "And if you are really here and this is not a dream, then I would love to be with you forever as well. I do not want to be away from you ever. You do not know how much I have missed you, Bryson. My life felt incomplete without you. Even if it was only a short time, I did not like it. The world is a much better place with you around."

This was no longer a nightmare for her, but a dream come true. She just hoped and prayed more than anything in the world that it was all really happening.

Chapter 21

"What is that noise?" Maisie twisted around, pulling herself away from Bryson ever so slightly. "What is happening?" Any sounds freaked her out now, she found it much too challenging. "Bryson, please!"

"You do not need to look." He attempted to shield her eyes, but she would not accept anything. Maisie no longer felt like she needed to be protected. She had already seen far too much, and she wanted to know what was going on. If this was something that she needed to worry about, then Maisie wanted to know. She had spent far too long not knowing everything and it ended up hurting her badly. "Maisie, stop..."

"Ray is dead?" She was not sure why this surprised her, but it did. Of course, now it made a lot of sense. He would not have stopped attacking her unless someone had done something to him. "What happened?"

Bryson did not need to answer that question because

Maisie could already see. As soon as he had seen Ray attacking Maisie he had acted immediately. He shot the arrow that slammed into Ray and prevented him from doing anything else to harm her. Bryson did not think twice. He saw the woman that he loved being harmed and he did what he could to keep her alive. But he did not want Maisie to think that he was a monster. He was not sure that she would like to see what he could do. Especially after today...

"Oh, wow, I see." Maisie gulped and nodded slowly. "Well, I suppose he would have killed me."

"Yes, that was what he wanted. He wanted to kill you. I only did what I could to save you."

Maisie allowed that to wash over her. Bryson had killed Ray to prevent him from hurting her. That made him a killer as well. But she did not see him as a bad person. She knew that he only did what he needed to in order to save her. She imagined that if the roles were reversed, she would have done the same thing for him. She would have done anything to keep him alive. He was her hero. Now and always.

"I only got here just on time as well," Bryson continued, knowing that he needed to justify himself in any way possible. "I only had the chance to shoot one arrow at him. Thankfully, it hit him."

Bryson would not have been able to forgive himself if he had arrived too late. He could not have another woman that he loved die, especially because there was nothing that he could have done this time and guilt would kill him. With Maisie, if he had been smarter, she would have stayed alive. It would have been the end of him.

"Yes, thankfully. You kept me alive, Bryson. You saved me. I am so grateful for that."

Bryson's men made a lot of noise over in the other direction so both him and Maisie turned to see. Maisie stiffened hard when she spotted what had created the commotion. She gasped so loudly that even Bryson began to panic along with her. She was simply not expecting to see Lauren's body so soon after she killed her. The woman was a sight to be seen, she had never looked so damn dreadful.

"Lauren is dead as well. Ray's sister," Bryson continued sadly. Yet a part of him was glad as well because he did not want anyone ever coming for Maisie again. The pain was too much. "Good riddance."

Maisie hung her head low, sadness encompassing her. She did not want to admit the truth to Bryson for fear of him seeing her differently, but she also could not lie to him. If he was really going to love her then he needed to know about every part of her, including the bits that he might not like so much. It scared Maisie to admit it aloud, but she knew that she had absolutely no choice in the matter.

"It was me," she said quietly, almost so quietly that Bryson did not hear her. "I was the one who killed Lauren." She shook her head sadly. "I did not mean to. It happened in the scuffle. She tried to kill me first and I snatched the dagger away from her. I took it to save myself and she fell forwards. It pierced her heart and I feel so terrible about it. I did not mean for her to die. I did not want anyone to die."

She sobbed hard into Bryson's chest, fearing that he would push her away now that he knew what she was capable of. She had not killed Lauren to save someone else, simply herself. It felt selfish somehow.

"I should have attacked her another way," she insisted, more to herself than anyone else at this point. "I should have never used the dagger to threaten her like that. I was not thinking straight, I was afraid. I just wanted her to get off of me. I did not think... I do not even know what happened. She fell. She fell..."

The memory of it was painful, it was agonizing, she did not want to think of Lauren and her death. She never wanted her to be there in her mind, feeling Lauren's blood all over her, watching her die, knowing that she was fully responsible. Yet Maisie also knew that it was just another memory that would sit with her forever. She had the memories from her past now, her memories of Bryson, and now the horrible memories in the middle of the forest which had only consumed of death and blood.

How was she going to mesh those memories together? How would she make it all feel alright inside of her? Right now, Maisie had no idea what she was going to do with the future that she had not planned for. Since she was supposed to die only a short while ago, what was supposed to happen next?

"You do not have to worry about what you did," Bryson reassured her. "I did bad things as well, but we did it to save ourselves from evil. We had to get away from Lauren and Ray..."

"Lauren was not Ray's sister," Maisie suddenly declared. "She was his lover. I saw them kissing."

Bryson's lips tightened into a thin line. "I had a feeling

that the pair of them were too close."

"Yes, well you were right." Maisie nodded a few times. "They wanted to kill me because they wanted my father's estate. I was the only thing standing in their way. Me and my memories. They were under the assumption that I would get them back eventually. It was to be their love nest and I could not ruin that."

"How did they have any rights to anything that ever belonged to your father?" Bryson asked, confused.

"Lauren was my stepmother. Married to my father, who she eventually murdered. She wanted to pin the murder on me which I suppose is the moment that I decided to run away. I am not too sure..."

"She told you all of this?" Bryson could not believe it. "Well, whatever happened, you can forget about this forest now. You do not ever have to worry about what happened in here ever again. It is gone."

"No," Maisie insisted immediately. "No, I do not want to forget anything ever again. It has taken me a long time to get my memories back. I cannot lose anything ever again. Even if the memories are ugly. It is those memories who make me who I am. I cannot be without myself any longer. I need me to live."

Bryson nodded along, taking everything that Maisie was saying on board, but not really allowing it to sink in. Not at first anyway. But after a while, it started to resonate with him, and he got it. He understood.

"Wait, what are you saying, Maisie?" he gasped. "That you have your memories back? All of them?"

"I do." She grinned from ear to ear. "I do have them

back. Some of the stuff came from Lauren and Ray. They sparked a lot, but a lot of it came at the end of my life. Or what I thought was going to be the end of my life anyway. It all started to come back to me then. I never knew my mother. She died when I was too young so she is someone that I will never know. That is why I have no memories of her. But the medallion... that is hers. That is why I have always kept it so close to me. My father was a wonderful man though. The absolute best. He raised me alone and did a great job of it." Maisie scowled. "Then Lauren came along and destroyed everything. Like a hurricane she ripped through my existence and wrecked everything. She killed my father and left me with the blame. As I ran away, I was robbed and I think that might be where I lost my memories. That is of course when you came into the picture. You saved my life."

She grinned from ear to ear, knowing that Bryson would be her hero forever. He saved her life there and here as well. That was why she could not forget anything. Not even the sickness. The vomit which dragged her out of the carriage and allowed her to see the truth. The truth of who she was with.

"I am stunned." Bryson did not know what to say. "I am stunned that you have your memories back. Happy, of course, I know that this is something you wanted, but... wow... what a set of memories."

"I know that they are not pretty," Maisie agreed. "I understand that it makes my whole life complicated. Not just the recent times when I have lost my memories, but before that as well. I know that this must make you think twice about me. About ever rescuing me again. It is very strange, I know."

"No." Bryson shook his head a little too loudly. "No, it is not strange. It is just a lot to take in. I always knew that you had a whole life behind you, but to hear it is something else."

Maisie cocked her head to one side and examined Bryson carefully. She was not sure what any of this meant. It was almost as if he could not accept her now, knowing the truth about her which was why he seemed so confused. There was nothing that she could do if that was the case. She would just have to walk away and go back to her home. She had memories of her home, but she was not sure that she could fit in now. She did not know what her old clan thought of her, but they had to have heard that she was a killer, and they would not want her around. Anyone who could do that to her father was not worthy. No one in her clan would like a girl with an evil side like that. If she was on the other side of things, nor would she.

Of course, if she had to, she could return and explain the truth. Try to make people understand her. Let them know that Lauren and Ray were the bad people. But knowing that they were dead as well, and that it was her fault did not help a lot, but Maisie would find a way. She had to. Since she had been through so much, and she had remained resilient the whole time, so she could do this as well if she needed to.

But Maisie knew that she did not want to. She would never be happy without Bryson, not really. She would survive if that was what life expected from her, but happiness would never come. Not ever.

Chapter 22

Bryson was sick with anxiety. He could hardly believe what he was hearing. Of course, it was wonderful news for Maisie to have her memories back, but what did that mean for them? He was almost too afraid to ask. Sure, they had declared their love for one another and had expressed a desire to be together forever, but that was just at the moment he had saved her life. Maybe, after time, she would not want him after all.

"I... I would still love for you to be my wife," he declared quietly, with some sadness in his tone. "But I do understand if you wish to wait, to give yourself time to decide what you want for the future. You may feel an aversion to your home right now because of how these people have made you feel, but the time may come when you want to return, to take your rightful place within your own clan. I cannot prevent that."

Bryson looked so downtrodden that it almost broke Maisie's heart. She took the underneath of his chin and brought his eyes up to meet hers. "Bryson. I do not need to have time to think. Despite everything that has happened, I am seeing with more clarity now and I know exactly what I want. My only worry is that the baggage I carry with me is going to be too much for you to handle. I understand if so."

Over the moon to hear that Maisie still wanted him, Bryson cupped her cheeks in his hands and pulled her towards him for a kiss. Their lips collided and made everything feel right with the world again. Bryson could not have been happier that he followed his instincts and he rescued Maisie from her captors. He knew now that he would never let her go with strangers again. No matter what.

"We must burn the bodies of the deceased," he told her softly. "But I will ensure that word is sent to your hometown to let them know that death came of them because of their murderous spree. I will also ensure that your name is cleared. It is not right for people to believe that you killed your father. Even if you do not wish to return, people should know the truth about Lauren and Ray. Is that alright?"

Maisie nodded eagerly. She did want her name cleared, she never wanted people to believe that she could do that to the man who raised her, who she loved so much, it was painful. Plus, people needed to understand what dangers could come with power. One wrong decision and life could end far too quickly. She did not know who would now take over ruling in her father's place, but she hoped that it would be someone who could make better choices with regards to who they got married to.

"That sounds perfect. Thank you, Bryson. I think that is the best solution for everyone."

Bryson and Maisie stayed behind as the bodies were burned to a crisp. Since Bryson was the one who had commanded that to happen, he felt it only right to remain while the act was carried out. Much as it sickened Maisie to witness it, she was glad to see this unfold with her own eyes as well. She needed the confirmation. There was nothing in the world that she wanted to be unsure of again.

It was closure, as well. The end of a terrible saga which had begun the day that Lauren started to worm her way into her father's life. It put everything to rest at long last, which had needed to happen for far too long. There would still be a lot of regrets surrounding it, a lot of things that Maisie wished could have been different, such as her mother remaining alive. But she could not regret everything too much because it had brought her to Bryson. She might have lived for her whole life not knowing him otherwise.

"I am looking forward to getting back home," Maisie mused as the smoke thickened above their heads. "I cannot wait to see all the people who I thought that I would be saying goodbye to forever. I am particularly looking forward to seeing Anice. I have missed her during the time I have been away."

"She is missing you too," Bryson confirmed. "Although you might have to prepare yourself. You may well be in trouble. She was very upset with you for leaving her without saying farewell."

Maisie let out a little laugh. "I will take whatever trouble she wants to throw my way. I know that I deserve it. If I had been thinking straight, then none of this would have happened."

"I simply hope that it does not happen again." Bryson turned to look at Maisie. "So, now that you have ruined your dress, when shall we replace your dress so that we can get married once more?"

Maisie glanced down at herself. There was no way that she could get hitched in this. Covered in blood and dirt, she looked more of a mess than she ever had done before. It was disgusting, she was horrified at herself. She knew that she would scare people. Much as this was a horror show, letting the world know what she had been through, she did not need reminding of it on the happiest day of her life.

"I would like to get married as soon as possible," Maisie agreed. "But not looking like I have been through hell. Our wedding day should only be about me and you and the love that we share. We have had too many happy times for it to be tainted. However, if I could get washed up as soon as we get back, and find something new to wear, even if it is not as fancy as this, I would marry you today."

Bryson was happy with that. "I do not mind what you are wearing. You will always be my angel. Yet if you change your mind while we are on the way back and want to start all over again, I will wait for you. Since I thought that I had lost you forever, there is no time waiting that will feel like too long."

Maisie leaned up and kissed Bryson delicately, allowing them both to swell up with love as they did. Maisie knew that Bryson was willing to be patient with her, but she was eager and keen to get this day back on track. This was meant to be the happiest day of their lives and she could not wait to fulfil it.

"Let us get back," she gushed happily at him. "I want to live this day as it was supposed to be lived."

"Never have I heard better words," Bryson laughed. "You really are the best thing that has ever happened to me, my angel. If you wish to have the day that we were destined to have then we shall go and do that."

On the ride home, Maisie leaned fully against her fiancé's back, smiling to herself in sheer happiness. She spent every moment that she could savoring every part of him. She knew that she would never take this man for granted. Knowing what it was like to live without him, she appreciated him even more.

This man is my hero, she thought to herself, loving how that felt. He always will be.

She had love, real love. Not all of her life had been lucky, just as Bryson's had not been, but now they were finally about to land on a real bit of luck that they hoped would stay with them forever more.

June was the first one to greet Maisie up on her return, which made sense since they had formed such a strong bond while Maisie was living in the castle. Despite the state of her, June flung her arms around her and hugged her tight. So grateful was she to have her friend back, she did not care about the mess.

"Please, never do that to me again," June begged. "I

was so afraid for you. I did not like it. I did not like those people at all, so I was pleased when Bryson made the decision to go after you."

June pulled back to finally drink in Maisie's appearance and gasped in horror. She looked hurt, there was bruising on her face and body from the fighting with both Lauren and Ray which stood out on her fair skin.

"Do not worry," Maisie immediately insisted, seeing what emotions June was racing through. "I know that I look terrible, but that is what happens when you must fight for your life. I was actually hoping that you would help clean me up as much as possible because I still want to get married today."

"Today?" June gushed in shock. "Do you not think that you have been through enough today? That is not to say that I cannot make you look beautiful because you are utterly filled with natural beauty, I just do not need you to push yourself. You must be utterly exhausted. You should rest..."

But Maisie's eyes danced and darted around with delight. "I have never felt more awake in my life, June. Finally, I have all of my memories back. That is the one good thing to have come from today. Finally, I know exactly who I am and what I want. I want to be married to Bryson as soon as possible."

"I have tried to tell her to rest as well," Bryson jumped in with an amused tone of voice. "But she is headstrong and knows exactly what she wants. Who am I to deny my angel her wedding when she wishes it?"

June could see the intense light within him again. He

had been deflated the moment that Maisie walked away from him, she feared that he would never recover again, but his love was back and so was he.

"Then I will see what I can do, Maisie." She took her friend's hand and led her inside the castle. "We must get you all cleaned up before Anice sees you. She will not understand that this is how a woman looks like when she is fighting for her life. I hope you will tell me everything that happened. I am intrigued..."

Maisie knew that she could trust June with her story, all of it, even the parts that she still feared made her look bad, so she would tell her everything while she was bathing and washing the nightmare of the day off of her. "I will tell you all of it, but it is not the prettiest of stories..."

"It is always the ugly tales that are more gripping," June laughed. "I prefer to hear yours. Especially since you are alive at the end of it. Alive and here to tell me all about it..."

"Not everyone got out of this story alive," Maisie admitted, thinking more of her parents as she made this statement, rather than Lauren and Ray. "But I am sure you have already guessed that."

"I am sure that a lot has been lost," June agreed. "But a lot has been gained as well. It is not always the easiest to remember that, but it is very much the truth. We have gained having you here."

Maisie agreed, because even without her parents, she had her memories of her father and who he really was keeping her going, and the medallion from her mother to keep them alive in her heart. And maybe a time would come when she would visit her father's kingdom once more to see if there were more trinkets, she could keep to have her family with her. But for now, she was satisfied with what she had. There were positive fragments in her story, and she could hold on to them at least.

Chapter 23

Anice could not wait until Maisie was dried and dressed before she saw her. The poor young girl had been on an absolute rollercoaster of emotions, from the happiness of the wedding to the upset when Maisie was taken away from her, so she needed to lay her eyes upon her to know that she was here for sure and staying as well. Maisie did not mind, she was keen to see Anice as well.

"Rose!" Anice ran up to Maisie and jumped into her arms. "I love you, Rose."

"Miss Anice, have you forgotten? Her name is Maisie. She has her memories back," June said.

But Maisie shook her head and laughed. "I will always be Rose to Anice. I do not mind that."

A tear ran down her face as they hugged so tightly it was like they would never let go, but for the first time in a very long time, it was a happy tear. She did not know what she was thinking when she left. How did she assume that she could be away from this little princess forever? Even if the tale that Lauren and Ray had been telling her was accurate, she could not have stayed away for good. It would not have worked.

"You are going to stay now, Rose?" Anice asked with nothing but concern in her voice. "You are really going to marry my father this time? Because I want you to be my step mommy. I do."

Huh, it was funny. To Maisie, the concept of a stepmother had always been a truly evil one because of Lauren, but that was what she would be to Anice once the wedding was complete. Maisie had not considered it this way at all, but now that she was thinking it she knew that she would do better. Anice deserved someone so much better than what she was given, and she could do that for her. She could be the loving stepmother, the one who cared about Anice as if she were her own child.

"I want that as well," she replied thickly through the emotion. "So, of course I am going to stay."

"And I have a feeling that there might be another child added into the mix soon," June declared with a wink. As she glanced at Maisie's belly, she grabbed on to it, almost protectively as if there was a life growing in there. "I am usually very good at sensing this sort of thing. So, a family, you will be."

Was that the reason she had become so sick on the journey? Because she was carrying a child who did not want to be ripped away from his or her father and sibling? It was all too possible, which made it even scarier the fact that Maisie almost walked away from everything without looking back. She nearly put herself in a terribly precocious situation. Thankfully, everything had worked out just as it should.

"Well that would be wonderful," Maisie said with a grin. "I would love nothing more. This castle and these lands are the only place where I would like to have my family, so that is wonderful news."

"Then why did you leave?" Anice demanded. "Why did you go with those people?"

Maisie was not sure how she could explain the complicated situation to such a young girl. It was all so messy. But she also did not want to be dishonest about anything. "I thought I owed them something. I was trying to do the right thing, but as it turned out the right thing would have made me very unhappy."

"The things that make us happy are the right thing." Anice nodded determinedly. "It makes sense."

If only the world was that straight forward. But Maisie hoped that here she would be able to make it as close as possible to that for Anice. She would not be able to shelter her from all of the pain in the world, that was impossible, but she would certainly give her a better life than she had been through. A better stepmother and role model at the very least. Not someone with murder always on the brain.

"Speaking of happiness," Maisie continued. "Do you think that you could help me pick out a dress for the wedding? The one that I was originally going to wear got all torn up as I came back here."

"Oh, no!" Anice smacked her hands to her cheeks in shock. "But you looked so beautiful in that dress."

"I think that I might even look better in one you pick

out for me. What do you think?"

"Are you sure about this?" June whispered as Maisie stepped back and let Anice loose on her clothing. "You are allowing a five-year-old girl to pick out the dress for the most important day of your life?"

"I am certain," Maisie nodded determinedly. "It is not about what I wear or even what I look like at all. It is about declaring my love for Bryson in front of the world and sealing myself to him forever more, exactly where I wish to be. I will be a part of his family, including Anice, and I want her to feel that."

June smiled at her kindhearted friend, noticing that her hands remained rested protectively on her stomach. She was sure that her instincts were right on this one, and that in some months' time, there would be another member of the clan. That would be exciting news for everyone, especially the MacGregor family.

"You are a lovely woman, Maisie," June told her in all seriousness. "We are all so lucky to have you here and I am so happy that you decided to return to us. Of course, I am very sorry about the circumstances that led up to it, but life is much better with you around. I love that we now get to keep you here for good."

Maisie held her friend's hand and smiled back. "There is nowhere else that I could ever be."

She knew that she meant that now, she meant it all because she had all of her inside of her brain. Everything that she had been through had brought her to this point, and it was perfect.

The wedding was beautiful. So much nicer and more poignant than Maisie ever could have imagined. Almost having the day snatched away from them made them appreciate it so much more. Especially Maisie. She now knew that her life could have been totally different, but this was what she wanted. In the sweet green dress that Anice had picked out for her as well, she felt like the person she was always meant to be. This version of her was always there inside of her, she had only just been set free.

All the guests loved it as well. There was not a dry eye in sight. Not a single person moaned that the wedding was back on again, they were all simply pleased for things to be back the way they were meant to be. Everyone had been sad to see Maisie go, she was the ray of sunshine that they all needed so desperately.

Bryson, as soon as the ceremony was over, felt compelled to make a speech. He needed everyone to see just how much this beautiful woman meant to him. The ceremony alone was not enough.

"Thank you everyone for joining me here today," he boomed over the silence, causing everyone to look at him. "I know that it has been a hard day because the initial wedding that we were supposed to have was cruelly shaken apart by people who we now know are liars and killers..." Gasps raised up around the room. It only occurred to Bryson at that moment everyone had not been fully aware of all the details pertaining to what happened when Maisie was away. Without wanting to get into all the details and make the day about Lauren and Ray who were definitely not welcome, he continued talking rapidly. "But we have regained our day and our love. We have been lucky, and that will always stay with me. I will always be grateful for what has happened here today, and I do hope that it offers you all an insight into how kind life can be. We can all get caught up sometimes in life being cruel, when that is not always the case, as this has proven. So, we can all remember what has happened here today when times are dark. Maisie will be our symbol of hope."

He held Maisie's hand and raised it into the sky causing everyone to erupt with glee. At least for today, they would all be caught up in positivity, into how incredible life could be, which was the sort of vibe that Maisie and Bryson knew that they always wanted to spread. Life did not get better than this.

The wedding soon rolled into a party. Everyone was in the mood for a celebration so it was clear that it would last into the night. Despite Maisie's long and tiring day, she wanted to join in anyway, but it came to a time, not long after Anice had crashed out asleep, that she felt the need for rest as well. There was no denying that the events of the day and the injuries she had sustained had taken it out of her.

"I am sorry," she whispered into her very happy husband's ear. "I think I might need to go to bed soon."

She thought that he might be upset with her because he wanted to continue on with the fun and he wished to have his new bride beside him at the same time, but he simply nodded and grinned at her.

"Oh, Maisie, my angel. I have been waiting to hear those words all night long from you. It is time for us to retire to our chambers. I do not believe that you have ever seen inside my bedroom before..." Maisie nodded realizing that was the truth. Anything that had ever occurred between them had been snatched moments in the room where she was sleeping at the time. "Well, now it is your room as well."

Excitement began to brew inside of Maisie as they said their goodnights to the rest of the clan, who clearly had no intention of ending the party any time soon, and it grew as they headed back inside the castle. She no longer felt the same weariness as before, it was more a tingle of thrill. Desire, perhaps. Maisie was happy to know that as Mrs. MacGregor, life was going to be a little different, and she was also thrilled to be allowed deeper into Bryson's life. But the feeling sparkling at her core was the intense throb of need. She wanted this man, even more so now that he was her husband.

"You know, June said to me that I might have a baby in my belly," she declared, testing the waters, just wanting to see how Bryson would react. "She believes that she is good at seeing these things."

Bryson span her around immediately and planted a kiss up on her lips. She could not stop herself from giggling at his glee. Thank goodness the idea of raising a child with her did not frighten him.

"I certainly hope so. I would love to have a baby with you," he declared proudly. "Otherwise, I will have to make sure that a baby is within you soon enough. I am ready for this family to grow and expand. I feel like I have so much love inside of me that we need children, just so I have somewhere for it to go."

Maisie's life suddenly got a lot bigger in her mind, and a lot more exciting as well...

Chapter 24

"Wow, your bedroom is amazing," Maisie gasped as soon as she saw the inside of the bedroom. "And you already have a lot of my clothing within here. You have been preparing for me."

"Of course, I have." His hands circled her waist, and he pulled her closer to him. "I have been preparing for this moment ever since I met you. I am simply grateful that we may now have this much needed time together. I was not sure that I would ever be able to step into this room again with you gone."

As Maisie span around and she laced her fingers through his, guilt raced through her body. She would have left him in a state of despair had she not returned to him. In doing what she thought was the right thing, she would have upset the people who truly cared about her. Never again would she make that mistake. This was the only place in the world that she wanted to be.

"Well, that is something that you shall never have to

worry about again."

Maisie lifted up on to her tip toes and kissed her hero once more, loving the way that his lips felt pressed against hers. His hands began to explore the contours of her body. Bryson had been tired throughout the day as well because it had been something of a rollercoaster, but not any longer. Not with this beautiful woman in his arms, he was far more awake than he had ever been. He had his angel back, life was perfect. And the night was about to get even better because her breathing was becoming labored...

"I love you," he whispered as he peeled her dress off of her gorgeously milky shoulders. "So much."

The dress tumbled to the ground, leaving Maisie with nothing else on. She had wanted to feel free during the ceremony and fully herself. This had done that for her. But seeing the delighted smirk on her husband's face, she now realized that no underwear had a secondary benefit as well.

"Oh wow, I really am so lucky." He pulled her back to him, loving every peak and dip of her curves. Her naked body pressed up against him was intoxicating. He could not get enough of her. "You are beautiful."

"Well, you are not so bad yourself, my handsome hero," she teased back. "But you are wearing far too much. I would like to see all of you. I do not think it fair to spend my wedding night naked and alone."

With those seductive words, Bryson was on fire. He watched in awe at the wonderful woman that Maisie had become, he could see a change within her now that she knew herself fully. He loved it. As she walked away from him backwards, keeping her eyes fixed up on him the entire time, his heart pounded vigorously against his chest. She slid back on to the bed sheets and indicated for him to take off his clothing.

He was not a self-conscious man, and he knew that he did not have to be in front of Maisie. She had fought to the death to be back with him and she loved him, every part of him. Still, there was a little bit of nervous excitement as he stripped himself down. The intensity of her exploring gaze up on him was a lot for him to handle. She was not shy about wanting to see every single part of him.

He gazed up on her just as intensely as he took everything off of his body. He had dressed himself so carefully before, wanting to look his absolute best for his bride, but as it turned out, all she wanted was him with nothing on. He loved that about her. She was just as cheeky as him.

"Well, you are a sight to behold," she declared as soon as he was naked. "I think I might need you over here with me because I already miss the feel of your body next to mine. I want you to hold me."

Bryson did exactly as Maisie commanded, noting to himself that this was the first time their bodies would connect with him not calling her Rosalyn. Not that it made as much difference as he thought it might. She was still his angel, and still incredibly familiar to him. He knew her in a very intimate and beautiful way and that was not going to change, whatever name he ended up calling her. A name did not express the sheer essence of his wife, and that was what he loved about her most of all.

He could not get enough of Maisie's body. His lips, his tongue, his fingers, all explored every part of her just as she was doing the same to him. It was deeply passionate and romantic. The intense love that they felt for one another shone through with every single second. Each moment they were connected to one another was more intense than the last. They could feel the rush coursing through their bodies, the passion bursting and about to explode. They could not get enough of one another and felt equally like this sensation would never end. As they took one another to the peak of the mountain, just before they tumbled over and fell into the abyss of pleasure, the love swelled and grew between one another.

Their marriage was destiny, it was meant to be, they were sure of it. This powerful chemistry and love did not come from nothing. It would last forever as well, they knew it with certainty. Nothing was ever going to come between them now. Nothing could wreck the wonder that they had become together.

And if there was a child on the way, or one about to come soon, then that would only make all of this even better. It would be something else that sealed them together for the rest of their lives.

"Laird MacGregor?" June's worried voice broke through the bedroom, waking him up from the most delightful slumber that he had ever experienced. It turned out that waking up with the love of his life beside him could do wonders for his mood. He did not want to leave the bed at all, but this sounded urgent.

"Yes, June?" he called back, trying to be loud enough for her to hear him without waking up Maisie.

"I hate to disturb you this early in the morning. But Maisie has a visitor. Someone who says that it is important. I did not think that you would want to deal with anyone after what happened yesterday, but he will not take no for an answer. I think it might be better if you get rid of him."

After what happened the day before, this put Bryson on edge. He did not like the idea of anyone else coming near Maisie, trying to take her away again, so without waking her, he slipped out of the bed and hurriedly got himself dressed in preparation for another confrontation. He could not understand why people from her past would not simply leave her alone. What could someone else want with her? If this was someone else after money that had belonged to her father, then there would be trouble.

"You did the right thing in coming to me," Bryson reassured June. "This is a situation that we must put an end to, once and for all. Was there any mention of Lauren and Ray? The people who arrived yesterday?"

"There was no mention of anyone," June admitted as she hurried behind Bryson. "I could not get any information from him. I was not sure how hard you would want me to push him."

"No, not at all, you must not put yourself in danger." Bryson's fists balled up by his side in anger. "I will put an end to this once and for all. Maisie is staying here with us. She has made her decision."

The man did not look like a threat as Bryson laid his eyes upon him. He did not have the same aura of evil as

Ray and Lauren, but that did not mean he could be trusted. Bryson would not let his guard down.

"I will not allow you to see my wife," Bryson began, potentially a little too aggressively, but he needed this stranger to know exactly where he stood. "Not until I know what you are doing here."

"I understand that." The man smiled back. It was a friendly smile that disarmed Bryson a little. "I am happy to explain to you why I am here, especially if you are the husband of lovely Maisie Ferguson."

"Right... I see..." This was a much nicer reception than Bryson had been expecting. "So, please come through to the grand hall with me and we can have a conversation in there. Please, June, would you request some beverages from the kitchen for me. I would not like our guest to be thirsty."

June nodded nervously, not quite sure what that comment meant. Would this be another bloodbath type of day where an increasing number of enemies were made, or would it be something much more pleasant for a change? They all needed to keep up the nice, happy spirit really.

As soon as she vanished, Bryson turned back to the man and waited for him to begin explaining.

"You see, Maisie's father, Duncan Ferguson, had a dying wish," the man began. "And it was all documented, but not discovered until Lauren, his wife, went missing, and we were informed of her betrayal and subsequent death. That is the moment people began to sort out his things. He has left a fortune to his daughter, money and treasure that he saved up throughout his lifetime to ensure that she could have a good life. It is only right that she be given the money. Whether she live here or at home."

"How are things at home?" Bryson immediately needed to know. "Are you in a time of turmoil?"

"We have been, but things are looking up. Now that Lauren and Ray are no longer in charge of anything, we can arrange for a good leader, for someone worthy of the role. Someone more like Duncan."

"You have someone in mind?" Bryson cocked his head to one side kindly. He had climbed down from his horse of anger very quickly. This man made him care. "Someone who you think can do this?"

"Yes, I think that we are going to be fine. But I have the fortune with me. I would like to hand it over to Maisie directly, if I may. I would like to explain to her that no one believes that she would ever do that to her own father. We never did believe it. She has always been more trustworthy than Lauren..."

"What is happening here?" As if she could sense herself being spoken about, Maisie appeared in the meeting room. "I know you... oh, my goodness, you are Jamie. How wonderful to see you!"

Bryson took a back seat as he allowed Maisie and Jamie to catch up. Now that he knew he had nothing to worry about, he was happy for them to talk. Of course, as he suspected, Maisie did not want to take the fortune easily, she wanted the clan to use it to help themselves recover from what Lauren and Ray did to them, but Jamie insisted that they had enough and this was Duncan's wishes. Bryson knew that Maisie would not use it to help herself though, she would do good with the money, she would use it to help others, and he would be with her every step of the way. Whatever his angel wanted. She was perfect and beautiful, sweet to the core, and he loved her entirely. Their life together was going to be amazing, he just knew it.

Épilogue

Nine months later...

"I have forgotten all about the pain already," Maisie declared as she looked into the depths of her son's beautiful eyes. "It is all worth it to hold this wonderful little man in my arms. He really is everything."

The closer that Maisie got to the end of her pregnancy, the more worried she became. A lot of women had died in childbirth, including Anice's mother and her own. She was scared that the same might happen to her, but it had not. She had gotten lucky once more and she was allowed to experience her happiness.

"Can you believe that this little boy is mine?" Tears flooded her eyes. Happy emotional tears. "I cannot believe it. I could not be happier than I am right now. Just look at his beautiful face."

He was the perfect mix of both Maisie and Bryson.

Just moments old, he already inhabited a lot of their features. Maisie's heart was warmer and bigger than it had ever been before. She had not needed to make more room inside her heart for her boy, instead her heart had grown tenfold.

"He really is perfect," Bryson agreed, almost as emotional as his wife. "But I can believe that he came from you. You have always been angelic, and our little boy is the same." Bryson stroked his head softly, allowing eons of love to wash through him. "What are we going to call our baby boy? We did not decide."

"I would like to name him after my father, if that is alright with you?" Maisie asked him. "I would like to honor my father. Keep him going because he deserves to live on, whereas the ones who took away his life do not. They are the ones that should be forgotten, should fade away in history..."

Maisie and Bryson never spoke of Lauren and Ray anymore, they did not mention their names because they were moving ever forwards with their lives, but the memories lived on. Particularly in Maisie. She would never forget because she did not want to forget anything. But they were not honored ever.

"Duncan," Bryson agreed. "I love that name. It suits our little man very much."

"You really like it?" Maisie was delighted. "You are not just saying that to please me?"

Bryson tossed his head back and laughed. "Of course, I am not just saying it. If it was a name that I really did not like, then I would let you know. But I love it. I think it fits his little face well."

Right at that moment, Maisie, Bryson, and little Duncan were interrupted by a very excitable big sister bursting into the room. Anice had tried her hardest to be patient, but she could not hold back any longer. It had taken forever for the baby to be born and she needed to spend every second with him that she could.

"Is he born yet?" she half screeched. "Do I get to hold him yet? I want to see him..."

The words tumbled away, and she fell into silence as Anice finally laid eyes on her baby brother. She was amazed by how sweet he was, by how tiny and fragile he appeared. She sat quietly beside him, snuggled into Maisie and she stared down at Duncan, her little pulse beating with delight.

"He is so sweet," she cooed. "I cannot believe how little he is. Is he really that small?"

"He sure is," Maisie replied, giggling at her innocence. "And his name is Duncan."

"Like your father." Anice nodded, proving that she knew more than anyone could have imagined. "I like that. Duncan is a nice name, and you had a nice father, just like me."

There had been a lot of screaming in the room where Duncan was born not long before. The agony tore through Maisie in a way that scared her to death. She really did think that it was going to kill her. But sitting here holding on to Duncan with one arm and Anice in the other, she knew that she would do it all over again. If her and Bryson decided that they wanted to have more children, she would go through anything for them. Her mother had not left her, she knew that now, she had sacrificed herself to give Maisie a chance to live. Thankfully, it was a life that she was living to the fullest, making the sacrifice worthwhile.

But there was no more screaming in the room now. Nothing but a peaceful quiet as the family sat together, enjoying their moment alone before everyone else in the clan would want to see the baby as well.

"I could stay here in this little room forever," Maisie said with a little emotional laugh. "It is so wonderful being with you all. I love my little family more than anything else in the world."

"But the party!" Anice blurted out, before she realized that was supposed to be a secret. "Oops, I mean..."

"It is alright," Bryson replied with amusement. "I was going to let Maisie know about the party in a moment anyway. We would not want her to be unprepared. The celebration needs her there too."

"You are holding a party for me?" Maisie was shocked. "Oh but, I do not know if I am ready for that."

"No one expects you to be the life and soul of the party," Bryson reminded her. "They just want you there. They want to celebrate you and little Duncan as well. They want you to know that we are all here for you. Raising a child is not always the easiest of tasks, but in this clan, everyone will be there for you."

Bryson knew that any of his people would do anything for Maisie, not only because they loved her, but because she had ensured that they were all set up for life. None of them were ever going to have to struggle for anything because she had insisted on helping every single one. She had proven herself to be the incredible woman that Bryson knew she would be the moment he spotted her in the forest.

To think that was a day when he had gone for a ride because he was worried about Anice. He was worried about her growing up without a mother. He rationalized it to himself by telling himself that she did not need one because of the clan, and perhaps that was true, but then he had seen his angel in the forest and he knew from that moment on that Anice wanted a mother like Maisie, even if she did not need one.

Fate had him out on his horse, destiny ensured that he found Maisie, and love had kept them together.

"I had a lot of help raising Anice," he continued. "I would not have been able to do it had I not. And you will get help too, even if you do not think that you need it. They will be there for you."

Maisie nodded, understanding what he was telling her. "I suppose I should get myself all organised then for the party. I will do my best for the wonderful people around me. I do love them all... although of course the people that I love the most are right here with me in this room."

Anice glanced up at her and smiled, Bryson stared at her like he always did, like she was the most beautiful woman on the planet, and her baby... well, Duncan was drifting off to sleep so his eyes were fluttering closed. She was more content than she thought possible, and it was perfect.

"I am enjoying this party," Maisie said quietly to June. "I

am so grateful for everyone here. The whole clan has been so nice to me. However, childbirth is exhausting. I do not know how much longer I can stay awake. Please, nudge me if I end up drifting off to sleep. I would not like to be rude..."

June laughed and hooked her arm over her best friend's shoulder. Maisie had given June enough to ensure that she never had to work again, but June loved working with the MacGregor family, so refused to stop. She also wanted to be around as much as possible with baby Duncan. He was adorable.

"If you fall asleep, I shall carry you up to bed myself. I cannot ask Bryson to do it because he has both children cuddled up in his arms. He is the doting daddy right now, so it is up to me."

Maisie glanced over to where June was pointing to see her family surrounded by her friends. It was the most beautiful sight that she had ever seen. She loved them all so much that she feared her heart might explode under the pressure of it. She did not know that she was capable of so much love.

"I really am lucky, do you not think so?" she murmured sleepily to June. "Being here, I have it all."

"Well, we are lucky to have you as well," June reminded her, as she often did. "It is a part of our happy ever after to have you here with us too. We would not be the same without you. The time when you left was a stark reminder of what it was like when you were not around and no one liked it. Not a soul."

Maisie rested her head on her friend's shoulder and allowed herself to drift off into just a little micro sleep. She needed an extra surge of energy to get her through the rest of the evening. This perfect evening with the people who had done nothing but welcome her and care for her, even when she was just a stranger to them all. They had changed her, and she had changed them as well, all for the best.

Maisie and Bryson had both suffered tragedy in their lives, suffered the sort of sadness that no one should ever have to go through, but they had worked through it to make themselves stronger, so now this happiness was wonderful. They had worked for it and they deserved it. Because of that, they would ensure to make the most of it, and they would do whatever they could to keep the children happy as well. With them to focus on, they knew that they could finally live that happy ever after, they really could have it all.

Content

CHAPTER 1 5
CHAPTER 2 13
CHAPTER 3 21
CHAPTER 4 29
CHAPTER 5 37
CHAPTER 6 45
CHAPTER 7 53
CHAPTER 8 61
CHAPTER 9 69
CHAPTER 10 77
CHAPTER 11 85
CHAPTER 12 93
CHAPTER 13 101
CHAPTER 14 109
CHAPTER 15 117
CHAPTER 16 125
CHAPTER 17 133
CHAPTER 18 141
CHAPTER 19 149

CHAPTER 20	157
CHAPTER 21	165
CHAPTER 22	173
CHAPTER 23	181
CHAPTER 24	189
ÉPILOGUE	197

Content

CHAPTER 1 5

CHAPTER 2 13

CHAPTER 3 21

CHAPTER 4 29

CHAPTER 5 37

CHAPTER 6 45

CHAPTER 7 53

CHAPTER 8 61

CHAPTER 9 69

CHAPTER 10 77

CHAPTER 11 85

CHAPTER 12 93

CHAPTER 13 101

CHAPTER 14 109

CHAPTER 15 117

CHAPTER 16 125

CHAPTER 17 133

CHAPTER 18 141

CHAPTER 19 149

CHAPTER 20	157
CHAPTER 21	165
CHAPTER 22	173
CHAPTER 23	181
CHAPTER 24	189
ÉPILOGUE	197

You may also be interested

No one should have messed with Laird Mason MacGregor.

After years of losses and struggles against the English, Mason only has his son and his clan left. And now he is about to lose everything.

With his son kidnapped and his castle threatened, Mason takes the path of revenge and kidnaps Lady Bethany Windsor, the daughter of his enemy.

Lady Bethany lives under the control of her father, who considers her a hindrance for being a woman. She feels alone in a wild country and with the only perspective of a marriage she does not want.

Until Laird MacGregor appears and changes everything.

Surrounded by enemies and with a man who should hate her, she finds a happiness that she did not think possible. But can Mason forget that they are enemies? Will he be able to believe in her innocence when they want to convince him that she is a traitor?

And most important, **can she love this badass Highlander?**

CPSIA information can be obtained
at www.ICGtesting.com
Printed in the USA
BVHW042204250521
608162BV00021B/234